(State) New York

Proposed Building Law for Medium Sized Cities

as drafted by a commission appointed pursuant to chapter 579, laws of

1892 of New York state - Issued June, 1893, by the Committee on

construction of buildings of the National board of fire underwriter

(State) New York

Proposed Building Law for Medium Sized Cities
as drafted by a commission appointed pursuant to chapter 579, laws of 1892 of New York state - Issued June, 1893, by the Committee on construction of buildings of the National board of fire underwriter

ISBN/EAN: 9783337385699

Printed in Europe, USA, Canada, Australia, Japan

Cover: Foto ©Andreas Hilbeck / pixelio.de

More available books at **www.hansebooks.com**

National Board of Fire Underwriters.

PROPOSED

Building Law for Medium Sized Cities

AS DRAFTED BY

A COMMISSION APPOINTED
PURSUANT TO CHAPTER 579, LAWS OF 1892 OF NEW YORK STATE.

MEMBERS OF THE COMMITTEE.

WM. J. FRYER AND CORNELIUS O'REILLY OF NEW YORK CITY, AND LEON STERN OF ROCHESTER.

Issued June, 1893, by the Committee on Construction of Buildings of the National Board of Fire Underwriters, and recommended for adoption by cities in the United States having no adequate Building Regulations.

JOHN W. MURRAY, *Chairman.*
GEO. R. CRAWFORD, New York.
M. BENNETT, JR., Hartford.   } *Committee.*
GEO. H. FROST, New Orleans.
JEFFREY BEAVAN, New York.

W. T. CHATTERLEY,
Stationer and Printer,
45 Liberty Street, New York.

AN ACT

To provide for the construction, regulation and inspection of buildings, and the more effectual prevention of fires and the better protection of life and property therein, in the several cities of the State, except the cities of New York and Brooklyn.

The People of the State of New York, represented in Senate and Assembly, do enact as follows:

SECTION 1. There are hereby enacted three classes of laws relating to the construction, regulation, survey and inspection of buildings to be known as title one, title two and title three of this act, which shall respectively apply to every city, according to its population, in this State, except the cities of New York and Brooklyn, which are hereby excepted from the operation of this act. Title one shall apply to all cities having a population exceeding seventy-five thousand inhabitants, namely, * * * * * . Title two shall apply to all cities having a population exceeding thirty thousand, but not exceeding seventy-five thousand inhabitants, and shall be deemed to include the cities of * * * * * . Title three shall apply to all cities having a population less than thirty thousand inhabitants, and shall include the cities of * * * * .

§ 2. When any village or town within this State shall hereafter be incorporated as a city, such city shall become subject to the provisions of title three of the laws hereby provided.

§ 3. When any city named in title two is hereafter shown by an enumeration of the inhabitants of this State to have a population in excess of seventy-five thousand inhabitants, then any said city having thus increased in population shall become subject to the provisions of title one of this act, and in similar manner any city named in title three, which may hereafter be shown by such enumeration to have increased in population beyond a total population of thirty thousand inhabitants, shall become subject to the provisions of title two of this act.

§ 4. The three classes of laws hereby provided in their application to the several cities are intended to and shall supersede any and all charter provisions or ordinances made thereunder relating to the construction, regulation, survey and inspection of buildings. So much of any and all acts as are inconsistent with the provisions of this act are hereby repealed, and any and all regulations or ordinances, or parts of same, made by the Common Council or other authorities of any city, to which one of the three classes of laws hereby provided is to apply, are hereby declared void and of no effect, so far as they or any of them may be inconsistent with the provisions of this act.

§ 5. It shall be the duty of the Mayor and Common Council, or of the Fire Department, as the case may be, in each of the several cities in this State, to provide for the enforcement of such one of the three classes of laws relating to buildings as by this act created is to apply to any said city. The expenses thereof shall be provided for in the same manner as other expenses of such city government.

§ 6. The provisions of this act shall not apply to buildings or structures belonging to or that may hereafter be erected by the United States or the State of New York.

TITLE I.

RELATING TO CITIES HAVING A POPULATION EXCEEDING SEVENTY-FIVE THOUSAND INHABITANTS.

§ 7. There is hereby created in each of the cities named in Section One of this Act, to which Title One is to apply, a "Department of Buildings," which shall be charged with the enforcement of the provisions of this act, as hereby provided for the survey and inspection of buildings.

§ 8. Within thirty days after this act shall take effect, the Mayor of said city shall nominate and, by and with the consent of the Common Council, appoint a Chief Officer for the Department of Buildings hereby created, who shall be called the Superintendent of Buildings. He shall be subject to removal by the Mayor after written charges have been preferred against him and after he has had an opportunity to be heard thereon. He shall hold his office for three years and until his successor be appointed, unless sooner removed, and shall be paid such salary as the proper municipal authorities shall determine. Said superintendent shall have power to appoint a deputy superintendent, inspectors, clerks and employees in such number and at such compensation as may be approved by the proper municipal authorities. The said department shall be furnished, at the expense of the city, with office room, and supplied with furniture, books, blanks, stationery and other supplies as may be necessary for the proper transaction of its business

§ 9. Within the fire limits of said city, as they now are or may hereafter be established by the Common Council of said city, no frame or wooden building shall hereafter be built, except as in this title authorized.

§ 10. The walls of all buildings, other than frame or wooden buildings, shall be constructed of stone, brick, iron or other hard incombustible material, and the several component parts of such buildings shall be as herein provided.

§ 11. No wall, structure, building, or part thereof, shall hereafter be built or constructed within said city, except in conformity with the provisions of this title. No building already erected or hereafter to be built, in said city, shall be raised, altered or built upon, in any manner that would be in violation of any of the provisions of this title.

§ 12. All excavations shall be properly guarded and protected by the person or persons causing the excavation to be made, so as to prevent the same from becoming dangerous to life or limb, and shall be sheet-piled where necessary to prevent the adjoining earth from caving in. Whenever an excavation of either earth or rock for building or other purposes shall be intended to be, or shall be, carried to the depth of more than ten feet below the street curb, the person or persons causing such excavation to be made shall at all times, from the commencement until the completion thereof, if afforded the necessary license to enter on the adjoining land, and not otherwise, at his or their own expense, preserve any adjoining or contiguous wall or walls from injury, and support the same by proper foundations, so that the said wall or walls shall be and remain practically as safe as before such excavation was commenced, whether the said adjoining or contiguous wall or walls are down more or less than ten feet below the street curb. If such excavation shall not be intended to be, or shall not be, carried to a depth of more than ten feet below the street curb, the owner or owners of such adjoining or contiguous wall or walls shall preserve the same from injury, and so support the same by proper foundations that it or they shall be and remain practically as safe as before such excavation was commenced, and shall be permitted to enter upon the premises where such excavation is being made for that purpose, when necessary. In case an adjoining party wall is intended to be used by the person or persons causing the excavation to be made, and such party wall is in good condition and sufficient for the uses of the adjoining building, then, and in such case, the person or persons causing the excavations to be made shall, at his or their own expense, preserve such party wall from injury and support the same by proper foundations, so that said party wall shall be and remain practically as safe as before the excavation was commenced. If the person or persons whose duty it shall be to preserve or protect any wall or walls from injury shall neglect or fail so to do, after having had a notice of twenty-four hours from the superintendent of buildings, then the superintendent of buildings may enter upon the premises and employ such labor and furnish such materials, and take such steps as, in his judgment, may be necessary to make the same safe and secure, or to prevent the same from becoming unsafe or dangerous, at the expense of the person or persons whose duty it is to keep the same safe and secure. Any party doing the said work, or any part thereof, under and by direction of the said superintendent, may bring and maintain an action against the person or persons last herein referred to, to recover the value of the work done and materials furnished, in and about the said premises, in the same manner as if he had been employed to do the said work by the said person or persons. When an excavation is made on any lot, and it is intended to use part of such excavation, on either the side or rear of the lot, as an area, or space for light and air, the person or persons causing such excavation to be made shall build at his or their own cost and expense, a retaining wall of sufficient strength to support the adjoining earth; and such retaining wall shall be carried to the height of the adjoining earth, and be properly protected or capped on top.

§ 13. Every building, except buildings erected upon wharves or piers on a water-front, shall have foundations laid not less than four feet below the surface of the ground, on the solid earth or on level surface of rock, or upon piles or ranging timbers when solid earth or rock is not obtainable for foundations. Piles intended for a wall, pier or post to rest upon, shall not be less than five inches in diameter at the smallest end, and shall be spaced not more than thirty-six inches on centres, or nearer if required by the superintendent of buildings, and shall be driven to a solid bearing. No pile shall be weighted with a load exceeding forty thousand pounds. The tops of all piles shall be cut off below the lowest water line. When required, concrete shall be rammed down in the interspaces between the heads of the piles to a depth and thickness of not less than twelve inches and for one foot in width outside of the piles. Where ranging and capping timbers are laid on piles for foundations, they shall be of hard wood, not less than six inches thick, and properly joined together and their tops laid below the water line. When crib footings of iron or steel are used below the water level, the same shall be entirely coated with coal tar, paraffine varnish, or other suitable preparation before being placed in position. When footings of iron or steel for columns are placed below the water level, they shall be similarly coated for preservation against rust. Foundation walls shall be construed to include all walls and piers built below the curb level or nearest tier of beams to the curb, to serve as supports for walls, piers, columns, girders, posts or beams. Foundation walls shall be built of stone or brick. If built of stone, they shall be at least eight inches thicker than the wall next above them to a depth of twelve feet below the curb level; and for every additional ten feet, or part thereof, deeper, they shall be increased four inches in thickness. If built of brick, they shall be at least four inches thicker than the wall next above them to a depth of twelve feet below the curb level; and for every additional ten feet, or part thereof, deeper, they shall be increased four inches in thickness. The footing or base course shall be of stone or concrete, or both, or of concrete and stepped-up brickwork, of sufficient thickness and area to safely bear the weight to be imposed thereon; if the footing or base course be of concrete, the concrete shall not be less than twelve inches thick; if of stone, the stones shall not be less than two by three feet, and at least eight inches in thickness for walls, and at least twelve inches wider than the bottom width of said walls, and not less than ten inches in thickness if under piers, columns, or posts, and at least twelve inches wider on all sides than the bottom width of said piers, columns or posts. All base stones shall be well bedded and laid crosswise, edge to edge. If stepped-up footings of brick are used in place of stone, above the concrete, the off-sets, if laid in single courses, shall each not exceed one and one-half inches, or if laid in double courses shall not exceed three inches, starting with the brickwork covering the entire width of the concrete, so as to properly distribute the load to be imposed thereon. If, in place of a continuous foundation wall, isolated piers are to be built to support the superstructure, where the nature of the ground and the character of the building make it necessary, inverted arches shall be turned between the piers, at least twelve inches thick and of the full width of the piers, and resting upon a continuous bed of concrete of sufficient area, and at least eighteen inches thick; or two footing courses of large stone may be used, the bottom course to be laid crosswise, edge to edge, and the top course laid lengthwise, end to end; or one course of concrete and one course of stone. The stone shall not be less than ten inches thick in each course, and the concrete shall not be less than eighteen inches thick, and the area of the lower course shall be equal to the area of the base course that would be required under a continuous wall, and the outside pier shall be secured to the second piers with suitable iron rods and plates. All stone walls twenty-four inches or less in thickness shall have at least one header extending through the wall in every three feet in height from the bottom of the wall, and in every four feet in length, and if over twenty-four inches in thickness, shall have one header for every six superficial feet on both sides of the wall, laid on top of each other to bond together, and running into the wall at least two feet. All headers shall be at least eighteen inches in width and eight inches in thickness and consist of good flat stones. No stone shall be laid in such walls in any other position than on its natural bed. Before the walls of buildings are carried up above the foundation walls, the cellars shall be connected with the street sewers. Should there be no sewer in the street, or if the cellars are below water, or below the sewer level, then provision shall be made by the owner to prevent water accumulating in the cellars to the injury of the foundations.

§ 14. In buildings where the space under the sidewalk is utilized, a sufficient stone or brick wall shall be built to retain the roadway of the street, and the side, end or party walls of such building shall extend under the sidewalk of sufficient thickness to such wall. The roofs of all vaults shall be of incombustible material. Openings in the roofs of vaults for the admission of coal or light shall be covered with glass to measure not more than four square inches each, set in iron frames or with iron covers having a rough surface, and rabbetted flush with the sidewalk. When areas are covered over, iron, or iron and glass combined, stone or other incombustible materials shall be used, and sufficient strength in such covering shall be provided to insure safety to persons walking on the same, and to carry the loads which may be placed thereon. Open areas shall be properly protected with suitable railings.

§ 15. The basement walls of dwelling houses, not over thirty-five feet in height, and not over twenty feet in width, nor more than forty-five feet in depth shall not be less than twelve inches thick, if of brick. The upper walls shall not be less than eight inches thick; but no party wall in any such building shall be less than twelve inches thick. The walls of all dwelling-houses, whether called tenement-houses, apartment-houses, flats, hotels or other buildings which are to be used for residence purposes, twenty-six feet or less in width between bearing walls, and also the walls of school-houses, which are hereafter erected, or which may be altered to be used as herein specified, over thirty-five feet in height and not over fifty feet in height, shall not be less than twelve inches thick above the foundation wall; but no wall shall be built having a twelve-inch thick portion measuring vertically more than fifty feet. If over fifty feet in height and not over sixty feet in height, the walls shall not be less than twelve inches thick above the basement, if a high stoop house, and not less than sixteen inches thick in the first story, if not a high stoop house. If over sixty feet in height, and not over seventy-five feet in height, the walls shall not be less than sixteen inches thick to the height of twenty-five feet, or to the nearest tier of beams to that height, and from thence not less than twelve inches thick to the top. If over seventy-five feet in height, and not over eighty-five feet in height, the walls shall not be less than twenty inches thick to the height of twenty feet, or to the nearest tier of beams to that height, thence not less than sixteen inches thick to the height of sixty feet, or to the nearest tier of beams to that height, and from thence not less than twelve inches thick to the top. If over eighty-five feet in height and not over one hundred feet in height, the walls shall not be less than twenty-four inches thick to the height of thirty-five feet, or to the nearest tier of beams to that height, thence not less than twenty inches thick to the height of seventy-five feet, or to the nearest tier of beams to that height, and from thence not less than sixteen inches thick to the top. If over one hundred feet in height and not over one hundred and fifteen feet in height, the walls shall not be less than twenty-eight inches thick to the height of twenty-five feet, or to the nearest tier of beams to that height, thence not less than twenty-four inches thick to the height of fifty feet, or to the nearest tier of beams to that height; thence not less than twenty inches thick to the height of ninety feet, or to the nearest tier of beams to that height, and from thence not less than sixteen inches thick to the top. If over one hundred and fifteen feet in height, each additional twenty-five feet in height or part thereof, next above the curb, shall be increased four inches in thickness, the upper one hundred and fifteen feet of wall remaining the same as specified for a wall of that height. All non-bearing walls of buildings hereinbefore in this section specified may be four inches less in thickness, provided, however, that none are less than twelve inches thick, except as hereinafter specified. Eight-inch brick partition walls may be built to support the beams in such buildings in which the distance between the walls is not over thirty-three feet; provided, that no clear span is over twenty-six feet; but no such partition wall shall be built having an eight-inch thick portion measuring vertically more than fifty feet. This clause shall not be construed to prevent the use of iron girders or iron girders and columns, or piers of masonry, for the support of the walls and ceiling over any room which has a clear span of more than twenty-six feet between walls. If the clear span is to be over twenty-six feet, then the bearing walls shall be increased four inches in thickness for every twelve and one-half feet or part thereof, that said span is over twenty-six feet. Whenever two or more dwelling-houses shall be constructed, not over twelve feet six inches in width, and not over fifty feet high, the alternate centre wall between any two such houses shall be of brick, not less than eight inches thick above the foundation wall; but no such wall shall have an eight-inch thick portion measuring vertically more than fifty feet; and the end of the floor beams shall be so separated that four inches of brick-work will be between the beams where they rest on the said centre wall. In no case shall either end of a floor beam or beams rest on stud partitions.

§ 16. The walls of warehouses, stores, factories, and stables, twenty-five feet or less in width between walls or bearings, shall not be less than twelve inches thick to the height of forty feet. If over forty feet in height, and not over sixty feet in height, the walls shall not be less than sixteen inches thick to the height of forty feet, or to the nearest tier of beams to that height, and not less than twelve inches thick from thence to the top. If over sixty feet in height, and not over seventy-five feet in height, the walls shall not be less than twenty inches thick to the height of twenty-five feet or to the nearest tier of beams to that height, and from thence not less than sixteen inches thick to the top. If over seventy-five feet in height and not over eighty-five feet in height, the walls shall not be less than twenty-four inches thick to the height of twenty feet, or to the nearest tier of beams to that height; thence not less than twenty inches thick to the height of sixty feet, or to the nearest tier of beams to that height, and thence not less than sixteen inches thick to the top. If over eighty-five feet in height and not over one hundred feet in height, the walls shall not be less than twenty-eight inches thick to the height of twenty-five feet, or to the nearest tier of beams to that height; thence not less than twenty-four inches thick to the height of fifty feet, or to the nearest tier of beams to that height; thence not less than twenty inches thick to the height of seventy-five feet, or to the nearest tier of beams to that height, and thence not less than sixteen inches thick to the top. If over one hundred feet in height, each additional twenty-five feet in height, or part thereof, next above the curb, shall be increased four inches in thickness, the upper one hundred feet of wall remaining the same as specified for a wall of that height. If there is to be a clear span of over twenty-five feet between walls, the bearing walls shall be four inches more in thickness than is in this section specified, for every twelve and one-half feet, or fraction thereof, that said walls are more than twenty-five feet apart. All buildings, not excepting dwellings, that are over one hundred and five feet in depth, without a cross wall, or proper piers or buttresses, shall have the side or bearing walls increased in thickness four inches more than is specified in the respective sections of this title for the thickness of walls for every one hundred and five feet, or part thereof, that the said buildings are over one hundred and five feet in depth. In all stores, warehouses and factories over twenty-five feet in width between walls in which there shall be brick partition walls, or girders supported on iron or wooden columns, or piers of masonry, the partition walls or girders, shall be so placed that the space between any two partition walls, or girders, shall not exceed twenty-five feet, and the iron or wooden columns, or piers of masonry, and girders, shall be made of sufficient strength and size to bear safely the weight and any lateral strain to be imposed upon them. In case iron or wooden girders, supported by iron or wooden columns, or piers of masonry, are substituted in place of brick partition walls, the building shall not exceed ten thousand feet area on the ground floor, except in case of fire-proof buildings which may be constructed as hereinafter provided for in section twenty-three of this title. In case the walls of any building are less than twenty-five feet apart, and less than forty feet in depth, or there are cross walls which intersect the wall, not more than forty feet distant or between the same, or piers or buttresses built into the walls, the interior walls may be reduced in thickness in just proportion to the number of cross walls, piers or buttresses, and their nearness to each other: provided, however, that this clause shall not apply to walls below sixty feet in height, and that no such wall shall be less than twelve inches thick at the top, and gradually increased in thickness by set-offs to the bottom; and the superintendent of buildings is hereby authorized and empowered to decide (except where herein otherwise provided for) how much the walls herein mentioned may be permitted to be reduced in thickness, according to the peculiar circumstances of each case, without endangering the strength and safety of the building. The walls of churches, theatres, foundries, machine-shops, car or stage-houses, armories, public markets not over two stories in height, and other buildings of a public character shall in no case be less than is in this act specified for warehouses; and said buildings shall have, in addition thereto, such piers or buttresses as, in the judgment of the superintendent of buildings, may be necessary to make a safe and substantial building. One-story structures, not exceeding a height of fifteen feet, may be built with eight-inch walls when the bearing walls are not more than nineteen feet apart, and the length of the eight-inch bearing wall does not exceed forty-five feet. Curtain walls of brick, built in between iron or steel columns, and supported wholly or in part on iron or steel girders, shall not be less than twelve inches thick for fifty feet of the uppermost height thereof, or to the nearest tier of beams to that measurement, in any building so constructed, and every lower section of fifty feet, or to the nearest tier of beams to such vertical measurement, or part thereof, shall have a thickness of four inches more than is required for the section next above it, down to the tier of beams nearest to the curb level; and thence downward the thickness of walls shall increase in the ratio prescribed in section thirteen of this title for the thickness of foundation walls.

§ 17. In all walls the same amount of materials may be used in piers or buttresses. Curtain walls may be made four inches less in thickness than is specified respectively for walls of dwellings, and buildings other than dwellings. If any horizontal section through any part of any bearing wall in any building shows more than twenty-five per centum area of flues and openings, the said wall shall be increased four inches in thickness for every ten per centum, or fraction thereof, or flue or opening area in excess of twenty-five per centum. All piers shall be built of stone or good, hard, well-burnt brick laid in cement mortar. Every pier built of brick, containing less than nine superficial feet at the base, supporting any beam, girder, arch or column on which a wall rests, or lintel spanning an opening over ten feet and supporting a wall, shall at intervals of not over thirty inches apart in height have built into it a bond stone not less than four inches thick, or a cast-iron plate of sufficient strength, and the full size of the piers. Isolated brick piers shall not exceed in height eight times their least dimensions. Stone piers or posts for the support of posts or columns above shall not be used in the interior of any building. Where walls or piers are built of coursed stone, with dressed level beds and vertical joints, the superintendent of buildings shall have the right to allow such walls or piers to be built of a less thickness than specified for brick work, but in no case shall said walls or piers be less than three-quarters of the thickness provided for brick work. In all brick walls every sixth course shall be a heading course, except where walls are faced with brick in running bond, in which latter case every sixth course shall be bonded into the backing by cutting the course of the face brick and putting in diagonal headers behind the same, or by splitting the face brick in half and backing the same with a continuous row of headers. All stone used for the facing of any building, and known as ashlar shall not be less than four inches thick. Stone ashlar shall be anchored to the backing and the backing shall be of such thickness as to make the walls (independent of the ashlar) conform to the thickness required by sections fifteen and sixteen of this title. Iron ashlar plates used in imitation of stone ashlar on the face of a wall shall be backed up with the same thickness of brick work as stone ashlar. Walls heretofore built for or used as party walls, whose thickness at the time of their erection was in accordance with the requirements of the then existing laws, but which are not in accordance with the requirements of this title, may be used if in good condition for the ordinary uses of party walls, provided the height of the same be not increased. In case it is desired to increase the height of existing party or independent walls, which walls are less in thickness than required under this title, the same shall be done by a lining of brick work to form a combined thickness with the old wall of not less than four inches more than the thickness required for a new wall corresponding with the total height of the wall when so increased in height. The said linings shall be supported on proper foundations and carried up to such height as the superintendent of buildings may require. No lining shall be less than eight inches in thickness, and all lining shall be laid up in cement mortar and thoroughly anchored to the old brick walls with suitable wrought iron anchors, placed two feet apart and properly fastened or driven into the old walls in rows alternating vertically and horizontally with each other, the old walls being first cleaned of plaster or other coatings where any lining is to be built against the same. In no case shall any wall or walls of any building be carried up more than two stories in advance of any other wall, except by permission of the superintendent of buildings. The front, rear, side and party walls shall be properly bonded together, or anchored to each other every six feet in their height by wrought-iron tie anchors, not less than one and a half inches by three-eights of an inch in size, and not less than twenty-four inches long. The walls of every building, during the erection or alteration thereof, shall be strongly braced from the beams of each story, and when required, shall also be braced from the outside, until the building is inclosed. The roof tier of wooden beams shall be safely anchored, with plank or joist, to the beams of the story below until the building is inclosed.

§ 18. The walls of all buildings below the curb level, or the first tier of floor beams nearest thereto, shall be laid in cement mortar, and the backing up of all stone ashlar shall also be laid up with cement mortar, or cement mortar and lime mortar mixed, but this shall not prohibit the parging of the back of the ashlar with lime mortar. All other walls built of brick or stone shall be laid in lime or cement mortar, or in lime and cement mortar mixed. In all walls that are built hollow, the same quantity of stone or brick shall be used in their construction as if they were built solid, as in this title provided, and no hollow wall shall be built unless the parts of same are connected by proper ties, either of brick, stone or iron, placed not over twenty-four inches apart. The inside four inches of all walls may be built of hard-burnt hollow clay or porous terra cotta blocks, properly tied and bonded into the wall, and of the dimensions of ordinary bricks. All exterior and division or party walls over fifteen feet high, excepting where such walls are to be finished with cornices, gutters or crown moldings, shall have parapet walls carried two feet above the roof, and shall be coped with stone, well-burnt terra cotta or cast iron. Recesses for stairways or elevators may be left in the foundation or cellar walls of all build-ings, but in no case shall the walls be of less thickness than the walls of the third story, unless reinforced by additional piers, with iron girders or iron columns and girders, securely anchored to walls on each side of recess. No chase for water or other pipes shall be made in any wall more than one-third of its thickness, and the chases around said pipe or pipes shall be filled up with solid masonry for the space of one foot at the top and bottom of each story. Recesses for alcoves and similar purposes shall in no case have less than eight inches of brick work at the back of such recesses, and provided that such recesses shall not be more than eight feet in width, and shall be arched over and not carried up higher than eighteen inches below the bottom of the beams of the floor next above. The aggregate area of recesses in any wall shall not exceed one-fourth of the whole area of the face of the wall on any story, nor shall any such recess be made within a distance of six feet from any other one in the same wall. In all furred or studded walls the course of brick above the under side and below the top of each tier of floor beams shall project the thickness of the furring or studs, to more effectually prevent the spread of fire. The walls and piers of all buildings shall be properly bonded and solidly put together with close joints filled with mortar. They shall be built to a line and be carried up plumb and straight. The walls of each story shall be built up the full thickness to the top of the beams above. All brick laid in non-freezing weather shall be well wet immediately before being laid. Walls or piers, or parts of walls or piers, shall not be built in freezing weather, and if frozen, shall not be built upon. The brick used in all buildings shall be good, hard, well-burnt brick. The sand used for mortar in all buildings shall be clean, sharp, sand, and shall not be finer than the standard samples kept in the office of the superintendent of buildings. Cement mortar shall be made of sand and cement in the proportion of not more than three parts of sand to one part of cement and shall be used immedi-ately after being mixed. Lime mortar shall be made of not more than four parts of sand to one part of lime, and shall not be used until thoroughly slaked. Cement and lime mortar shall be made of one part of lime, one part of cement and three parts of sand to each. Concrete for foundations shall be made of one part of cement, two parts of sand and five parts of small, clean broken stone, or one-half of the five parts may be clean gravel and the other half small, clean broken stone, all carefully mixed.

§ 19. Every building hereafter altered to be occupied as a hotel, and every building hereafter erected or altered to be occupied as a lodging-house, and every tenement-house, apartment-house and dwelling-house five stories in height, or having a basement and four stories in height above a cellar, hereafter erected or altered to be occupied by one or more families on any floor above the first, shall have the first floor above the cellar or lowest story constructed fire-proof with iron or steel beams and brick arches. The stairs from the cellar or lowest story to the fire-proof floor next above, when placed within any such building, shall be inclosed with brick walls. The opening through the brick wall of such inclosure into the lowest story shall have an iron door or a tin-covered wooden door constructed as hereinafter described in section thirty of this title, and shall be self-closing. Every such building exceeds five stories in height, or having a basement and five stories in height above a cellar, shall be constructed as in this section before described, and shall also have the halls and stairs inclosed with twelve-inch brick walls. Eight-inch brick walls not exceeding fifty feet in their vertical measurement, may inclose said halls and stairs, and be used as bearing walls where the distance between the outside bearing walls does not exceed thirty-three feet and the area between the said brick enclosure walls does not exceed two hundred superficial feet. The floors, stairs and ceilings in said halls and stairways shall be made of iron, brick, stone or other hard incombustible materials, excepting that the flooring and sleepers underneath the same may be of wood and the treads and handrails of the stairs may be of hard wood, provided that where wooden treads are used the underside of the stairs shall be entirely lathed with iron or wire lath and plastered thereon, or covered with metal. At least one flight of such stairs in each of said buildings shall extend to the roof, and be inclosed in a bulkhead built of fire-proof materials. When the said halls and stairways are placed centrally in or back from the front line of the building, a connecting fire-proof hallway inclosed with brick walls shall be provided on the first story and extend to the street. In every building hereafter erected, all the walls or partitions forming interior light or vent shafts shall be built of brick, or such other fire-proof materials as may be approved by the superintendent of buildings. The walls of all light or vent shafts, whether exterior or interior, hereafter erected, shall be carried up not less than three feet above the level of the roof. Eight-inch brick and six-inch and four-inch hollow tile partition walls of hard-burnt clay, or porous terra cotta, may be built, not exceeding in their vertical portion a measurement of fifty, thirty-six and twenty-four feet respectively, and in their horizontal measurement a length not exceeding seventy-five feet, unless strengthened by proper cross walls, piers or buttresses bonded into same. All such walls shall be carried on proper foundations, or on iron girders, or on iron girders and columns or piers of masonry. One line of fore and aft partitions in the cellar or lowest story, supporting stud partitions above, in all buildings over eighteen feet between bearing walls in the cellar or lowest story, hereafter erected, shall be constructed of brick, not less than eight inches thick, or piers of brick with openings arched over below the underside of the first tier of beams, or piers of brick, or iron columns, with wooden girders when the first tier of floor beams are of wood, or iron or steel girders when the floor beams are of iron or steel, or rolled iron or steel beams of sufficient strength to span the entire width for the first tier of beams may be used, and the stairs shall be inclosed by a suitable brick wall carried up to the top of the tier of beams nearest the curb line. Fore and aft stud partitions and such other main stud partitions as may be required by the superintendent of buildings, which may be placed in the cellar or lowest story of any building, shall have good solid stone or brick foundation walls under the same, which shall be built up to the top of the floor beams or sleepers, and the sills of said partitions shall be of locust or other suitable hard wood; but if the walls are built five inches higher of brick than the top of the floor beams or sleepers, any wooden sill may be used on which the studs shall be set. Fore and aft stud partitions that rest directly over each other shall run through the wooden floor beams and rest on the plate of the partition below, and shall have the studding filled in solid between the uprights to the depth of the floor beams with brick laid in mortar or other suitable in-combustible materials. All girders supporting the first tier of wooden beams in buildings shall be supported by brick piers, or iron, locust or other suitable hard wood, posts of sufficient strength on proper foun-dations. The floor of the cellar or lowest story in every dwelling-house, tenement-house, apartment-house, lodging-house and hotel hereafter erected, shall be concreted with suitable materials not less than three inches thick. The ceiling over every cellar or lowest floor in dwelling-houses more than three stories in height, when the beams are of wood, shall be lathed with metal lath and plastered thereon with two coats of brown mortar of good materials. When wood wainscoting is used, in any building hereafter erected, the surface of the wall or partition behind such wainscoting shall be plastered down to the floor line, and any intervening space between the said plastering and wainscoting shall be filled in solid with incombustible material.

§ 20. Openings for doors and windows in all buildings, except as otherwise provided, shall have good and sufficient arches of stone, brick or terra cotta, well built and keyed with good and sufficient abutments, or lintels of stone as follows: For an opening not more than four feet in width, the lintel shall not be less than eight inches in height; and for an opening not more than six feet in width, the lintel shall not be less than twelve inches in height; and for an opening exceeding six feet in width, and not more than eight feet in width, the lintel shall be the full thickness of the wall to be supported, and not less than fifteen inches in height. Every stone lintel over such opening six feet or less in width, in all walls, shall not be less than four inches thick, and shall have a bearing at each end of not less than five inches on the wall. On the inside of all openings in which the stone lintel shall be less than the thickness of the wall to be supported, there shall be a good timber lintel on the inside of the stone lintel, which shall rest at each end not more than three inches on any wall, and shall be chamfered at each end, and shall have a double row-lock or bonded arch turned over the timber lintel. Or the inside lintel may be of cast-iron, and in such case stone blocks or cast-iron plates shall not be required at the ends where the lintel rests on the walls, provided the open-ing is not more than six feet in width.

§ 21. The height of all walls shall be measured from the curb level at the centre of the building to the top of the highest point of the roof beams in the case of flat roofs, and for high-pitched roofs the average of the height of the gable shall be taken as the highest point of the wall. In case the wall is carried on iron girders or iron girders and columns, or piers of masonry, the measurement, as to height, may be taken from the top of such girder. When the walls of a structure do not adjoin the street, then the average level for the ground adjoining the walls may be taken instead of the street curb level for the height of such structure. The width of build-ings, for the purposes of this title, shall be determined by the way the beams are placed. The lengthwise of the beams may be considered and taken to be the widthwise of the building, and the bearing walls are those walls on which the beams or trusses rest.

§ 22. In every building used as a dwelling-house, tenement-house, apartment-house, lodging-house, school-house or hotel, each floor shall be of sufficient strength in all its parts to bear safely upon every superficial foot of its surface seventy pounds; and if to be used for office purposes, not less than one hundred pounds upon every superficial foot; if to be used as a place of public assembly, one hundred and twenty pounds; and if to be used as a store, factory, warehouse, or for any other manufacturing or commercial purpose, one hundred and fifty pounds and upwards upon every superficial foot. Every floor shall be of sufficient strength to bear safely the weight to be imposed thereon in addition to the weight of the materials of which the floor in composed. The roof of all buildings shall be proportioned to bear safely fifty pounds upon every superficial foot of their surface in addition to the weight of the material composing the same. Every column, post or other vertical support shall be of sufficient strength to bear safely the weight of the portion of each and every floor depending upon it for support in addition to the weight required as before stated to be supported safely upon said portions of said floors. The dimensions of each piece or combination of materials required shall be ascertained by computation, according to the rules given in Haswell's Mechanics' and Engineers' Pocket Book, except as may be otherwise provided for in this title. The strength of all columns and posts shall be computed according to Gordon's Formula, and the crushing weights in pounds, to the square inch of section, for the following named materials, shall be taken as the coefficients in said formula, namely: Cast iron, eighty thousand; wrought or rolled iron, forty thousand; rolled steel, forty-eight thousand; white pine and spruce, three thousand five hundred; pitch or Georgia pine, five thousand; American oak, six thousand. The breaking strength of wooden beams and girders shall be computed according to the formula in which the constants for tranverse strains for central loads shall be as follows, namely: Hemlock, four hundred; white pine, four hundred and fifty; spruce, four hundred and fifty; pitch or Georgia pine and American oak, five hundred and fifty; and for wooden beams and girders carrying a uniformly distributed load the constants will be double. The factors of safety shall be as one to four for all beams, girders and other pieces, subject to a transverse strain; and as one to four for all posts, columns and other vertical supports when of wrought iron or rolled steel, and as one to five for other materials, subject to a compressive strain; and as one to six for tie-rods, tie-beams, and other pieces subject to a tensile strain. Good, solid, natural earth shall be deemed to safely sustain a load of four tons to the superficial foot, or as otherwise determined by the superintendent of buildings, and the width of the footing courses shall be at least sufficient to meet this requirement. In computing the weight of walls, a cubic foot of brick work shall be deemed to weigh one hundred and fifteen pounds. Sandstone, white marble, granite and other kinds of building stone shall be deemed to weigh one hundred and sixty pounds per cubic foot. The safe-bearing load to apply to good brick work shall be taken at eight tons per superficial foot, when good lime mortar is used; eleven and one-half tons per superficial foot when good lime and cement mortar mixed is used; and fifteen tons per superficial foot when good cement mortar is used. The safe-bearing load to apply to good concrete shall be taken at eleven tons per superficial foot. Every temporary support placed under any structure, wall, girder or beam, during the erection, finishing, alteration or repairing of any building or structure, or any part thereof, shall be of sufficient strength to safely carry the load to be placed thereon. In all warehouses, storehouses, factories, workshops, and stores where heavy materials are kept or stored, or machinery introduced, the weight that each floor will safely sustain upon each superficial foot thereof, shall be estimated by the owner or occupant, or by a competent person employed by the owner or occupant. Before any building hereafter erected is occupied and used, in whole or in part, for any of the purposes aforesaid, and before any building, erected prior to the passage of this act but not at such time occupied for any of the aforesaid purposes is occupied or used, in whole or in part, for any of said purposes, the weight that each floor will safely sustain upon each superficial foot thereof, shall be ascertained and posted in a conspicuous place on each story of the building to which it relates. The weight placed on any of the floors of any building shall be safely distributed thereon, and the superintendent of buildings may require the owner or occupant of any building, or of any portion thereof, to redistribute the load on any floor, or to lighten such load, as he may direct, where he may deem the same to be necessary for the protection of life and property. No person shall place or cause or permit to be placed on any floor of any building any greater load than the safe load thereof, as correctly estimated and ascertained as herein provided. If the superintendent of buildings shall have cause to doubt the correctness of said estimate he is empowered to revise and correct the same, and for the purpose of such revision the officers and employes of said department of buildings may enter any building and remove so much of any floor or other portion thereof as may be required to make necessary measurements and examinations, and any expense necessarily incurred in removing any floor or other portion of any building for the purpose of making any examination herein provided for shall be paid by the city treasurer upon the requisition of the superintendent of buildings, out of the fund paid over to him under the provisions of section fifty-four of this act. Such expenses shall be a charge against the person or persons by whom or on whose behalf said estimate was made, and shall be collected in an action to be brought in the name of said department of buildings or fire department, as the case may be, against said person or persons, and the sum so collected shall be paid over to the said city treasurer to be deposited in said fund in reimbursement of the amount paid as aforesaid.

§ 23. Every building hereafter erected to be used as a hotel or school-house, the height of which exceeds sixty feet, and every building hereafter erected or altered to be used as a hospital, asylum, or institution for the treatment of persons, the height of which exceeds forty-five feet, and every other building the height of which exceeds seventy-five feet, except grain elevators and buildings for which specifications and plans have been heretofore submitted to and approved by the proper authorities, shall be built fire-proof; that is to say, they shall be constructed with walls of brick, stone, iron or other hard, incombustible material, in which wooden beams or lintels shall not be placed, and in which the floors and roofs shall be of materials similar to the walls. The stairs and staircase landings shall be built entirely of brick, stone, iron, or other hard, incombustible materials. No woodwork or other inflammable material shall be used in any of the partitions, furrings, or ceilings in any such fire-proof buildings, excepting, however, that the doors and windows, and their frames, the trims, the casings, the interior finish when filled solid at the back with fire-proof material, and the floor boards and sleepers directly thereunder, may be of wood. In all fire-proof buildings the following rules shall be observed:

1. All cast-iron, wrought-iron, or rolled steel columns shall be made true and smooth at both ends, and shall rest on iron or steel bed plates, and have iron or steel cap plates, which shall also be made true. All iron or steel trimmer beams, headers and tail beams, shall be suitably framed and connected together, and the iron girders, columns, beams, trusses and all other iron work of all floors and roofs shall be strapped, bolted, anchored and connected together and to the walls, in a strong and substantial manner. Where beams are framed into headers, the angle irons which are bolted to the tail beams shall have at least two bolts for all beams over seven inches in depth, and three bolts for all beams twelve inches and over in depth, and these bolts shall not be less than three-quarters of an inch in diameter. Each one of such angles or knees, when bolted to girders, shall have the same number of bolts as stated for the other leg. The angle iron in no case shall be less in thickness than the header or trimmer to which it is bolted; and the width of angle in no case shall be less than one-third of the depth of beam, excepting that no angle knee shall be less than two and a half inches wide, nor required to be more than six inches wide. All wrought iron or rolled steel beams eight inches deep and under shall have bearings equal to their depth, if resting on a wall; nine to twelve-inch beams shall have a bearing of ten inches, and all beams more than twelve inches in depth shall have bearings of not less than twelve inches if resting on a wall. Where beams rest on iron supports, and are properly tied to the same, no greater bearings shall be required than one-third of the depth of the beams. Iron or steel floor beams shall be so arranged as to spacing and length of beams that the load to be supported by them, together with the weights of the materials used in the construction of the said floors shall not cause a deflection of the said beams of more than one-thirtieth of an inch per linear foot of span; and they shall be tied together at intervals of not more than eight times the depth of the beam.

2. Under the ends of all iron or steel beams where they rest on the walls, a stone or cast-iron template shall be built into the walls. Said template shall be eight inches wide, in twelve-inch walls, and in all walls of greater thickness said template shall be twelve inches wide, and such templates, if of stone, shall not be in any case less than two and one-half inches in thickness, and no template shall be less than twelve inches long.

3. All brick or stone arches placed between iron or steel floor beams shall be at least four inches thick, and have a rise of at least one and a quarter inches to each foot of span between the beams. Arches of over five feet span shall be properly increased in thickness, as required by the superintendent of buildings, or the space between the beams may be filled in with sectional hollow brick of hard-burnt clay, porous terra cotta, or some equally good fire-proof material, having a depth of not less than one and one-quarter inches to each foot of span, a variable distance being allowed of not over six inches in the span between the beams. The said brick arches

shall be laid to a line on the centers, with close joints, and the bricks shall be well wet, and the joints filled with cement mortar in proportions of not more than two of sand to one of cement by measure. The arches shall be well grouted and pinned or chinked with slate, and keyed. The bottom flanges of all wrought-iron or rolled steel floor beams, and all exposed portions of such beams below the abutments of the floor arches shall be entirely encased with hard-burnt clay or porous terra cotta, or with wire metal lath properly secured and plastered on the under side. The exposed sides and bottom plates or flanges of wrought-iron or rolled steel girders supporting iron, steel or wooden floor beams, or supporting floor arches or floors, shall be entirely encased in the same manner.

§ 24. All iron or steel lintels shall have bearings proportionate to the weight to be imposed thereon, but no lintel used to span any opening more than ten feet in width shall have a bearing less than twelve inches at each end, if resting on a wall, but if resting on an iron post, such lintel shall have a bearing of at least six inches at each end, by the thickness of the wall to be supported. If the posts are to be party posts in front of a party wall, and are to be used for two buildings, then the said posts shall not be less than sixteen inches on the face by the thickness of the wall above, and if the party wall be more than sixteen inches thick, then the post shall be the thickness of the wall on the face. Intermediate posts may be used, which shall be sufficiently strong, and the lintels thereon shall have sufficient bearings to carry the weight above with safety. When the lintels or girders are supported at the ends by brick walls or piers they shall rest upon cut granite or blue stone blocks at least twelve inches thick, or upon cast-iron plates of equal strength by the full size of the bearings. In case the opening is less than twelve feet, the stone blocks may be six inches in thickness, or cast-iron plates of equal strength by the full size of the bearings may be used. This requirement shall not apply to the cast-iron lintels used at the back of stone lintels over openings not exceeding six feet in width. In all cases where the girder carries a wall and rests on brick piers or walls, the bearings shall be sufficient to support the weight above with safety. No cast-iron lintel or beam shall be less than three-quarters of an inch in thickness in any of its parts. Iron beams or girders used to span openings more than sixteen feet in width, upon which walls rest or upon which floor beams are carried, shall be of wrought-iron or rolled steel and of sufficient strength, or cast-iron arch girders may be used having a rise of not less than one inch to each foot of span between the bearings, with one or more wrought-iron tie-rods of sufficient strength to resist the thrusts, well fastened at each end of the girder. All lintels or girders placed over any opening in the front, rear or side of a building, or returned over a corner opening, when supported by brick or stone piers or iron columns, shall be of iron or steel and of the full breadth of the wall supported. In all buildings hereafter erected or altered, where any iron or steel column or columns are used to support a wall or part thereof, whether the same be an exterior or an interior wall, excepting a wall fronting on a street, and columns located below the level of the sidewalk which are used to support exterior walls or arches over vaults, the said column or columns shall be either constructed double, that is, an outer and an inner column, the inner column alone to be of sufficient strength to sustain safely the weight to be imposed thereon, or such other iron or steel column of sufficient strength and so constructed as to secure resistance to fire, may be used as may be approved by the superintendent of buildings. Iron posts in front of party walls shall be filled up solid with masonry and made perfectly tight between the post and walls to prevent effectually the passage of smoke or fire. Cast-iron posts or columns which are to be used for the support of wooden or iron girders or brick walls, not cast with one open side or back, before being set up in place, shall have a three-eighths of an inch hole drilled in the shaft of each post or column, by the manufacturer or contractor furnishing the same, to exhibit the thickness of the castings; and any other similar sized hole or holes which the superintendent of buildings, or his duly authorized representatives, may require shall be drilled in the said posts or columns by the said manufacturer or contractor at his own expense. Iron posts or columns cast with one or more open sides and backs shall have solid iron plates on top of each to prevent the passage of smoke or fire through them from one story to another, excepting where pierced for the passage of pipes. No cast-iron post or column shall be used in any building of a less average thickness of shaft than three-quarters of an inch, nor shall it have an unsupported length of more than twenty times its least lateral dimensions or diameter. No wrought-iron or rolled-steel column shall have an unsupported length of more than thirty times its least lateral dimension or diameter, nor shall its metal be less than one-fourth of an inch in thickness. All cast-iron, wrought-iron and steel columns shall have their bearings faced smooth, and at right angles to the axis of the column; and when one column rests upon another column, they shall be securely bolted together. Where columns are used to support iron or steel girders carrying curtain walls, the said columns shall be of cast-iron, wrought-iron or rolled steel, and on their exposed outer and inner surfaces be constructed to resist fire by having a casing of brick work not less than four inches in thickness and bonded into the brick work of the curtain walls, or the inside surfaces of the said columns may be covered with an outer shell of iron having an air space between; and the exposed sides of the iron or steel girders shall also be similarly covered in and tied and bonded. When the thickness of the curtain walls is twelve inches the girders for the support of same shall be placed at the floor line of each story, commencing at the line where the thickness of twelve inches starts from, and when the thickness of such walls is sixteen inches the girders shall be placed not farther apart than every other story, at the floor line, commencing at the line where the thickness of sixteen inches start from, provided that at the intermediate floor line a suitable tie of iron or steel shall rigidly connect the columns together horizontally; and that the ends of the floor beams do not rest upon the said sixteen-inch walls. When the curtain walls are twenty inches or more in thickness and rest directly on the foundation walls the ends of the floor beams may be placed directly thereon, but at or near the floor line of each story ties of iron or steel incased in the brick work shall rigidly connect the columns together horizontally. The iron arches, or the usual light castings connecting the columns of an iron front of a building, shall be filled in from the soffits to the sills on each upper story with brick work not less than eight inches thick, or hollow burnt clay blocks not less than eight inches thick and carried through the open back columns to the same upper level, the brick work or blocks to rest on the plates within the columns.

§ 25. Rolled iron or steel beam girders, or riveted iron or steel plate girders used as lintels or as girders, carrying a wall or floor or both, shall be so proportioned that the loads which may come upon them shall not produce strains in tension or compression upon the flanges of more than twelve thousand pounds for iron, nor more than fifteen thousand pounds for steel per square inch of the gross section of each of such flanges, nor a shearing strain upon the web-plate of more than six thousand pounds per square inch of section of such web-plate, if of iron, nor more than seven thousand pounds if of steel; but no web-plate shall be less than one-quarter of an inch in thickness, Rivets in plate girders shall not be less than five-eighths of an inch in diameter, and shall not be spaced more than six inches apart in any case. They shall be so spaced that their shearing strains shall not exceed nine thousand pounds per square inch of section, nor their bearing exceed fifteen thousand pounds per square inch, on their diameter, multiplied by the thickness of the plates through which they pass. The riveted plate girders shall be proportioned upon the supposition that the bending or chord strains are resisted entirely by the upper and lower flanges, and that the shearing strains are resisted entirely by the web-plate. No part of the web shall be estimated as flange area, nor more than one-half of that portion of the angle iron which lies against the web. The distance between the centers of gravity of the flange areas will be considered as the effective depth of the girder. Before any girder, as before mentioned, to be used in any building shall be so used, the architect or the manufacturer of or contractor for it shall, if required so to do by the superintendent of buildings, submit for his examination and approval a diagram showing the loads to be carried by said girder, and the strains produced by such load, and also showing the dimensions of the materials of which said girder is to be constructed to provide for the said strains; and the manufacturer or contractor shall cause to be marked upon said girder, in a conspicuous place, the weight said girder will sustain, and no greater weight than that marked on such girder shall be placed thereon. Before any iron or steel beam, lintel or girder intended to span an opening over ten feet in length in any building, shall be used for supporting a wall, the manufacturer or founder thereof, or the owner of said building, shall have the said beam, lintel or girder inspected, and if required by the superintendent of buildings, shall have the same tested by actual weight or pressure thereon, under the direction and supervision of an inspector authorized by the superintendent of buildings. Said manufacturer, founder or owner shall notify the superintendent of buildings, in writing, of the time when, and the place where said inspection and test may be made, and said inspector shall cause the weight which each of said beams, lintels or girders will safely sustain, to be properly stamped or marked in a conspicuous place thereon, and no greater weight shall be put or placed upon any beam, lintel or girder than that stamped or marked thereon by said inspector. The deflection of a cast-iron beam, lintel or girder, under an applied test of double the weight to be carried, shall not exceed one-fiftieth of an inch to the foot of span, and said beam, lintel or girder shall return to its original shape after the test. In case any iron or steel beam, girder or lintel, or any iron or steel column, shall be rejected by said inspector as unfit or insufficient to be used for the purpose proposed, the same shall not be used for such purpose, in or upon or about any building or part thereof. All iron work or steel work used in any building shall be of the best material and made in the best manner, and properly painted with oxide of iron and linseed oil paint before being placed in position, or coated with some other equally good preparation, or suitably treated for preservation against rust.

§ 26. All wooden beams or other timbers in the party wall of every building built of stone, brick or iron, shall be separated from the beam or timber entering in the opposite side of the wall by at least four inches of solid mason work. No wooden floor beams nor wooden roof beams used in any building, exceeding three stories in height, hereafter erected, shall be of a less thickness than three inches. All wooden trimmer and header beams shall not be less than one inch thicker than the floor or roof beams on the same tier, where the header is four feet or less in length; and where the header is more than four feet and not more than fifteen feet in length, the trimmer and header beams shall be at least double the thickness of the floor or roof beams, or shall each be made of two beams forming such thickness properly spiked or bolted together, and when the header is more than fifteen feet in length wrought iron flitch plates of proper thickness and depth shall be placed between two wooden beams suitably bolted together to and through the iron plates in constructing the trimmer and header beams; or wrought-iron or rolled-steel beams of sufficient length may be used. Every wooden beam, except header and tail beams, shall rest at one end four inches in the wall, or upon a girder as authorized by this title. All wooden floor and wooden roof beams shall be properly bridged with cross-bridging and the distance between bridging or between bridging and walls shall not exceed eight feet. Every wooden header or trimmer more than four feet long, used in any building, shall be hung in stirrup-irons of suitable thickness for the size of the timbers. No timber shall be used in any wall of any building where stone, brick or iron is commonly used, except lintels, as hereinbefore provided. The ends of all wooden floor and roof beams, where they rest on brick walls, shall be cut to a bevel of three inches on their depth, so that in case of fire they may fall without injury to the walls. All wooden beams shall be trimmed away from the flues, whether the same be a smoke, air or any other flue, the trimmer beam to be eight inches from the inside face of a flue in a straight way and four inches from the outside of a chimney breast, and the header two inches from the outside face of the flue. All fire-places shall have trimmer arches to support hearths and the said arches shall be at least sixteen inches in width, measured from the face of the chimney breast, and at least one foot longer on each side than the width of the fire-place opening, and they shall be constructed of brick, stone or burnt clay. Wooden centering under trimmer arches shall be removed before plastering the ceiling underneath. Each tier of beams shall be anchored to the side, front, rear or party walls at intervals of not more than six feet apart, with good, strong wrought-iron anchors of not less than one and a half inches by three-eighths of an inch in size well fastened to the side of the beams by two or more nails made of wrought-iron at least one-fourth of an inch in diameter. The ends of beams resting upon girders shall be butted together, end to end, and strapped by wrought-iron straps of the same size and distance apart, and in the same beam as the wall anchors, and shall be fastened in the same manner as said wall anchors, or they may lap each other at least twelve inches and be well spiked or bolted together where lapped. Where the beams are supported by girders, the girders shall be anchored to the walls and fastened to each other by suitable iron straps. Every pier and wall, front or rear, shall be well anchored to the beams of each story, with the same size anchors as are required for sidewalls, which anchor shall hook over the second beam. Each tier of beams front and rear, opposite each pier, shall have hard wood or Georgia pine anchor strips dove-tailed into the beams diagonally, which strips shall cover at least four beams, and be one inch thick and four inches wide, but no such anchor strips shall be let in within four feet of the center line of the beams; or wooden strips shall be nailed on the top of the beams and kept in place until the floors are being laid. Wooden columns supporting wooden girders and wooden floor beams and wooden roof beams, in all buildings more than two stories in height, shall each have cap and base plates of iron not less than one inch thick, and of proper size and shape. Said wooden columns, when placed one over another, shall not bear upon any wooden girder, but shall bear directly upon each other, or shall have between the iron plates suitable iron dowels passing through the girders. All timbers and wood beams used in any building shall be of good, sound material, free from rot, large and loose knots, shakes, or any imperfection whereby the strength may be impaired, and be of such size and dimensions as the purposes for which the building is intended require.

§ 27. All fire-places and chimneys in stone or brick walls in any building hereafter erected, and any chimney or flues hereafter altered or repaired, without reference to the purpose for which they may be used, shall have the joints struck smooth on the inside, except when lined on the inside with pipe. No pargeting mortar shall be used on the inside of any fire-place, chimney or flue. The fire-backs of all fire-places hereafter erected shall be not less than eight inches in thickness of solid masonry. The stone or brick work of all smoke flues, and the chimney shafts of all furnaces, boilers, bakers' ovens, large cooking ranges and laundry stoves, and all flues used for a similar purpose shall be at least eight inches in thickness. If there is a cast-iron or burnt clay pipe built inside of the same, with one inch air space all around it, then the stone or brick work inclosing such pipes shall not be less than four inches in thickness. All smoke flues of smelting furnaces or of steam boilers, or other apparatus which heat the flues to a high temperature, shall be built with double walls, with an air space between them, the inside four inches to be of fire-brick or fire-clay slabs or blocks laid in fire mortar, to the height of twenty-five feet from the bottom. All smoke flues shall extend at least three feet above a flat roof and at least two feet above a peak roof, and shall be coped with well-burnt terra-cotta, stone or cast-iron. In all buildings more than three stories in height hereafter erected every smoke flue shall be lined on the inside with cast-iron or well-burnt clay, or fire-proof terra-cotta pipe, from the bottom of the flue, or from the throat of the fire-place, if the flue starts from the latter, and carried up continuously to the extreme height of the flue. The ends of all such lining pipes shall be made to fit close together, and the pipe shall be built in as the flue or flues are carried up. Each smoke pipe shall be inclosed on all sides with not less than four inches of brick work properly bonded together. All stone or brick hot-air flues and shafts shall be lined with tin, galvanized iron or burnt clay pipes. No wooden casing, furring or lath shall be placed against or cover any smoke flue or metal pipe used to convey hot air or steam. No smoke pipe shall pass through any floor or roof of any building. No stove pipe in any building with wooden or combustible floors, ceilings or partitions, shall enter any flue unless the said pipe shall be at least twelve inches from either the said floors, ceilings or partitions, unless the same is properly protected by a metal shield, in which case the distance shall not be less than six inches. In all cases where stove pipes pass through stud or wooden partitions of any kind, they shall be guarded by either a double collar of metal with at least three inches of air space and holes for ventilation, or by a soap-stone or burnt clay ring not less than three inches in thickness and extending through the partition. Where laundry stoves, hot water, steam, hot air or other furnaces are used in any building, the smoke pipe leading therefrom must be kept not less than eighteen inches from the floor beams or ceiling unless the same is properly protected by a metal shield, when the distance shall not be less than nine inches. In all cases where such pipe passes through a wood or stud partition it shall be protected by a thimble with eight inches of brick work around it or a double collar of metal with at least six inches air space, and holes for ventilation. Tin or other metal flues, or pipes used or intended to be used to convey heated air, shall be inclosed with a brick or stone at least four inches in thickness, or other hard incombustible materials. Horizontal pipes and hot air pipes in stud partitions, shall be built in the following manner: The pipes shall be double, that is, two pipes, one inside the other, at least one-half inch apart, and there shall be a space of three inches between the pipe and stud on each side; or if a single pipe is used the inside faces of said studs shall be well lined with tin plate and the outside faces covered with brick, iron, lath or slate. Horizontal hot-air pipes shall be kept six inches below the floor beams or ceiling; if the floor beams or ceiling are plastered and protected by a metal shield, then the distance shall not be less than three inches. In cases where hot-air pipes pass through a wood or stud partition, they shall be guarded by either a double collar of metal, with two inches air space and holes for ventilation, or they shall be surrounded by brick work at least four inches in thickness. All flues in every building shall be properly cleaned and all rubbish removed, and the flues left smooth on the inside upon the completion of all buildings. No chimney shall be started or built upon any floor or beam of wood. In no case shall a chimney be corbeled out more than eight inches from the wall, and in all such cases the corbeling shall consist of at least five courses of brick. Where chimneys are supported by piers, the piers shall start from the foundation on the same line with the chimney breast, and shall not be less than twelve inches on the face, properly bonded into the walls. No chimney shall be cut off below, in whole or in part, and supported by wood, but shall be wholly supported by stone, brick or iron. All chimneys which shall be dangerous in any manner whatsoever, shall be repaired and made safe, or taken down. Iron cupola chimneys of foundries shall extend at least ten feet above the highest point of any roof within a radius of fifty feet of such cupola, and be covered on top with a heavy wire netting. No brick oven, coffee roaster or any other brick structure to contain fire shall be placed on a wooden floor or a floor supported by wooden beams in any building. All smoke-houses hereafter erected or constructed shall be built fire-proof, and the door and window openings in same shall be provided with iron or tin covered wooden doors or shutters. Before any building hereafter erected is occupied or used, in whole or in part, for wood-working purposes, and before any building erected prior to the passage of this act, but not at such time occupied or used, in whole or in part, for any aforesaid purposes, is so occupied or used, a fire-proof vault shall be constructed in connection therewith, of sufficient capacity to contain all shavings, sawdust, chips and other light combustible refuse resulting from such manufacture. All such combustible refuse shall be daily removed to the vault, and shall not be allowed to accumulate within or near the building unless stored in the vault to be provided as herein required.

§ 28. No steam pipe shall be placed within two inches of any timber or woodwork unless the timber or woodwork is protected by a metal shield, then the distance shall not be less than one inch. All steam pipes passing through floors and ceilings or lath and plastered partitions shall be protected by a metal tube one inch larger in diameter than the pipe, and the space shall be filled in with mineral wool, asbestos or other incombustible material. All wooden boxes or casings inclosing steam pipes, and all covers to recesses shall be lined with iron or tinplate. All brick hot-air furnaces shall have two covers, with an air-space of at least four inches between them; the inner cover of the hot-air chamber shall be either a brick arch or two courses of brick laid on galvanized iron or tin, supported by iron bars; the outside cover, which is the top of the furnace, shall be made of brick or metal supported by iron bars, and so constructed as to be perfectly tight, and shall not be less than four inches below the ceiling or floor beams. The walls of the furnace shall be built hollow in the following manner: One inner and one outer wall, each four inches in thickness, properly bonded together, with an air-space of not less than three inches between them. Furnaces must be built at least four inches from all woodwork. All cold air boxes shall be made of metal, brick or other incombustible material, for a distance of at least three feet from the furnace. All portable hot-air furnaces shall be kept at least two feet from any wooden or combustible partition or ceiling unless the partitions and ceilings are properly protected by a metal shield when the distance shall not be less than one foot. Wooden floors under any portable furnace shall be protected by a suitable stone, or a course of bricks well laid in mortar. Said stone or bricks shall extend at least two feet beyond the furnace in front of the ash-pan. All such register boxes shall be made of tin-plate with a flange on the top to fit the groove in the frame, the register to rest upon the same; there shall be an open space of two inches on all sides of the register-box, extending from the under side of the border to and through the ceiling below. The said opening shall be fitted with a tight tin casing, the upper end of which shall be turned under the frame. When a register-box is placed in the floor over a portable furnace, the open space on all sides of the register-box shall not be less than three inches. When only one register is connected with a furnace said register shall have no valve. Stoves shall not be placed nearer than twenty inches to any unprotected woodwork. Floors under all stoves shall be protected by a covering of incombustible material. Where a kitchen range is placed near a wooden stud partition, the studs shall be cut away and framed two feet higher and one foot wider than the range, and filled in to a line with said stud partition with brick or fire-proof blocks and plastered thereon. In cases where hot water, steam, hot air or other heating appliances or furnaces are hereafter placed in any building, or flues or fire-places are changed or enlarged, due notice shall first be given to the superintendent of buildings by the contractor or superintendent of said work.

§ 29. No gas, water or other pipes which may be introduced into any building shall be let into the beams unless the same be placed within thirty-six inches of the end of the beams; and in no building shall the said pipes be let into the beams more than two inches in depth. Every building other than a dwelling-house, hereafter erected, and all factories, hotels, churches, theaters, school-houses and other buildings of a public character now erected in which gas or steam is used for lighting or heating, shall have the supply pipes leading from the street mains provided each with a stop-cock placed in the sidewalk at or near the curb, and so arranged as to allow of shutting off at that point. All gas brackets shall be placed at least three feet below any ceiling or woodwork, unless the same is properly protected by a shield; in which case the distance shall not be less than eighteen inches. No swinging or folding gas brackets shall be placed against any stud partition or woodwork. Gas lights placed near window curtains or any other combustible material shall be protected by a proper shield. Every electric wire for furnishing light, heat or power, led into any building from the outside thereof, shall be arranged with suitable appliances to cut off the current on the outside of the building. All wires placed inside of buildings, whether in connection with æreal or underground wires and carrying electrical currents, shall be properly insulated. The superintendent of buildings shall make rules and regulations governing the method of construction, operation, location, arrangement, insulation and use of all electrical wires, appliances or currents, tor furnishing light, heat or power which may be introduced into or placed in any building. Said rules and regulations shall, as far as practicable, be made to conform to those which now are or hereafter may be prescribed by the Underwriters' Association of New York State. In no case shall any such wire, appliances and currents be introduced into any building, nor shall any of them be used or operated until the superintendent of buildings shall have first examined into and found that the method of construction, location, arrangement, insulation and use of such electrical wires, appliances and currents are safe and in accordance with the rules and regulations made by him, as aforesaid.

§ 30. Every building which is more than two stories in height above the curb level, except dwelling-houses, hotels, school-houses and churches shall have doors, blinds or shutters made of iron, hung to iron hanging frames or to iron eyes built into the wall, on every window and opening above the first story thereof, excepting on the front openings of buildings fronting on streets or open spaces which are more than thirty feet in width. Or the said doors, blinds or shutters may be constructed of pine or other soft wood of two thicknesses of matched boards at right angles with each other, and securely covered with tin, on both sides and edges, with folded lapped joints, the nails for fastening the same being driven inside the lap; the hinges and bolt or latches shall be secured or fastened to the door or shutter after the same has been covered with the tin, and such doors or shutters shall be hung upon an iron frame, independent of the woodwork of the windows and doors, or two iron hinges securely fastened in the masonry; or such frames, if of wood, shall be covered with tin in the same manner as the doors and shutters. All occupants of buildings shall close the said shutters, doors and blinds at the close of the business of each day. All shutters opening on fire-escapes, and at least one row, vertically, in every three rows on the front window openings above the first story of any building, shall be so arranged that they can be readily opened from the outside by firemen. All rolling iron or steel shutters hereafter placed in the first story of any building shall be counter-balanced so that said rolling shutters may be readily opened by the firemen. All windows and openings above the first story of any building may be exempted from having shutters by the written consent of the superintendent of buildings. Where openings in interior brick walls are fitted with fire-proof doors or shutters to prevent the spread of fire between different buildings, or between parts of any building, the said doors or shutters shall be closed at the close of the business of each day by the occupant or occupants of the building having use or control of the same.

§ 31. In any building in which there shall be any hoistway or freight elevator or well-hole not inclosed in walls constructed of brick or other fire-proof material, and provided with fire-proof doors, the openings thereof through and upon each floor of said building, shall be provided with and protected by a substantial guard or gate, and with such good and sufficient trap-doors, with which to close the same, as may be directed and approved by the superintendent of buildings; and when, in his opinion, automatic trap-doors are required to the floor openings of any uninclosed freight elevator, the same shall be so constructed as to form a substantial floor surface when closed, and so arranged as to open and close by the action of the elevator in its passage either ascending or descending. The said superintendent shall have exclusive power and authority within said city to require the openings of hoistways or hoistway shafts, elevators and well-holes in buildings to be inclosed or secured by trap-doors, guards or gates and railings. Such guards or gates shall be kept closed at all times, except when in actual use, and the trap-doors shall be closed at the close of the business of each day by the occupant or occupants of the building having the use or control of the same. In all buildings hereafter erected the roof, immediately over the hoistway, elevator or well-hole, shall be covered with a skylight of suitable size, glazed with thin sheet glass, so as to allow smoke, gases and flame to readily force their way through when a fire occurs. The glass in every such skylight shall have immediately under the same a wire netting, unless the glass contains a wire netting within itself, or what is known as wire glass. All elevators hereafter placed in any building, except fire-proof buildings, shall be inclosed in suitable walls of brick, or with a suitable frame-work of iron and burnt-clay filling, or of such other fire-proof material and form of construction as may be approved by the superintendent of buildings. If the inclosure walls are of brick, laid in cement mortar, and not used as bearing walls, they may be eight inches in thickness for not more than fifty feet of their uppermost height, and increasing in thickness four inches for each lower fifty feet, portion or part thereof. Said walls or construction shall extend through and at least three feet above the roof. All openings in the same shall be provided with fire-proof doors and made solid for three feet above the floor level, and with grill openings above. Elevators may be put in the well-hole of stairs, in buildings, without such brick or fire-proof inclosures, where the stairs are inclosed in brick or stone wall, and the stairs are constructed as specified in Section Nineteen of this Title. Elevators may also be placed in any stairwell or open court of any building erected prior to the passage of this act, under a permit therefor from the superintendent of buildings, but the frame work and inclosure of any such elevator shall be constructed of fire-proof materials. The foregoing requirements as to brick or fire-proof shafts shall include all dumb-waiters except such as do not extend through more than three stories in dwelling-houses. The roofs over all inclosed elevators shall be made of fire-proof materials, with a sky-light at least three-fourths the area of the shaft, made of thin sheet glass, set in iron frames, as hereinbefore in this section described, including wire netting underneath the glass of the sky-light or the use of wire glass. Immediately under the machinery at the top of every elevator shaft hereafter placed in any building in said city there shall be provided and placed a substantial grating or screen of iron, of such construction as shall be approved by the superintendent of buildings. The superintendent of buildings shall cause an inspection of passenger elevators as often as once a year. Any repairs found necessary upon inspection of any elevator shall be made without delay by the owner or person having the care or control of the same, and in case defects are found to exist which would endanger life by the continued use of such elevator, then, upon notice from the superintendent of buildings, the use of such elevator shall cease, and it shall not again be used until a certificate shall be first obtained from said superintendent that such elevator has been put in safe order and is fit for use. No person shall employ or permit any person to be in charge of running any passenger elevator who is under eighteen years of age or who does not possess proper qualifications therefor. Every freight elevator or lift shall have a notice posted conspicuously thereon as follows: Persons riding on this elevator do so at their own risk. Every elevator in any building erected to be occupied, or now occupied, as a hotel, shall, within six months after the passage of this act, be inclosed in suitable walls constructed and arranged as in this section required for elevators hereafter placed in buildings, unless under the provisions of this section such elevator might have been placed in said building without such inclosing walls.

§ 32. If a mansard or any other roof having a pitch of over sixty degrees be placed on any building, except a wooden building, or a dwelling-house not exceeding thirty-five feet in height, it shall be constructed of iron rafters and lathed with iron on the inside and plastered, or filled in with fire-proof material not less than three inches thick, and covered with metal, slate or tile. All exterior cornices and gutters of all buildings hereafter erected, except wooden buildings, shall be of fire-proof material. All fire-proof cornices shall be well secured to the walls with iron anchors, independent of any wood work. Where a wall is finished with a cornice of stone, terra cotta or similar material, the greatest weight of the material of such cornice shall be on the inside of the face of the wall, so that the cornice shall firmly balance upon the wall. In all cases the walls behind metal cornices shall be carried up to the planking of the roof, and where the cornice projects above the roof the walls shall be carried up to the top of the cornice, and the party walls shall in all cases extend up above the planking of the cornice and be coped   All exterior wooden cornices that may now be or that may hereafter become unsafe or rotten shall be taken down, and if replaced shall be constructed of fire-proof material. All exterior cornices of wood or gutters that may hereafter be damaged by fire to the extend of one-third shall be taken down, and if replaced shall be constructed of fire-proof material; but if not damaged to the extent of one-third, the same may be repaired with the same kind of material of which they were originally constructed. Bulkheads used as inclosures for elevators and coverings for the machinery of elevators and all other bulkheads, including the bulkheads of all dwelling-houses hereafter erected or altered, may be constructed of hollow fire-proof blocks or of wood covered with not less than two inches of fire-proof material or filled in the thickness of the studding with such material, and covered on the outside with metal, including sides and edges of doors. Covers on top of water tanks placed on roofs, may be of wood covered with tin. The planking and sheathing of the roof of every building hereafter erected, except a wooden building, shall in no case be extended across the front, rear, side, end or party wall thereof. Every such building and the tops and sides of every dormer-window thereon shall be covered and roofed with slate, tin, copper, iron, gravel or such other quality of fire-proof roofing as the superintendent of buildings, under his certificate, may authorize, and the outside of the frames of every dormer-window hereafter placed upon any building as aforesaid shall be of fire-proof material. No wooden building within the fire limits more than two stories or over twenty feet in height above the curb level to the highest part thereof, which shall require roofing, shall be roofed with any other roofing or covering, except as aforesaid. Nothing in this section shall be construed to prohibit the repairing of any shingle roof, provided the building is not altered in height. All buildings shall have scuttles or bulkheads, covered with fire-proof material, with ladders or stairs leading thereto. No scuttle shall be less in size than two by three feet. All sky-lights having a superficial area of more than twelve square feet, placed in any building, shall have the sashes and frames thereof constructed of iron and glass. Every fire-proof roof hereafter placed on any building shall have, beside the usual scuttle or bulkhead, a sky-light or sky-lights of a superficial area equal to not less than one-fiftieth the superficial area of such fire-proof roof. All buildings shall be kept provided with proper metallic leaders for conducting water from the roofs in such manner as shall protect the walls and foundation of said buildings from injury. In no case shall the water from the said leaders be allowed to flow upon the sidewalk, but the same shall be conducted by pipe or pipes to the sewer. If there be no sewer in the street upon which such buildings front, then the water from said leader shall be conducted by proper pipe or pipes below the surface of the sidewalk to the street gutter.

§ 33. It shall not be lawful for the owner or owners of any brick dwelling-house with eight-inch walls, or of any wooden building already erected that has a peaked roof, to raise the same for the purpose of making a flat roof thereon, unless the same be raised with the same kind of material as the building, and unless such new roof be covered with some of the articles mentioned in Section Thirty-two of this Title, and provided that such building, when so raised, shall not exceed forty feet in height to the highest part thereof. All such buildings must exceed twenty-five feet in height to the peak of the roof before the said alteration and raising. If any such building shall have been built before the street upon which it is located is graded, or if the grade is altered, such building may be raised or lowered to meet the requirements of such grade. No frame building more than two stories in height, now used as a dwelling, shall hereafter be raised or altered to be used as a factory, warehouse or stable. No brick or wooden building shall be enlarged or built upon unless the exterior walls of said addition or enlargement be constructed of fire-proof materials; provided, however, that such brick or wooden buildings may be raised, lowered or altered, under the same circumstances and in the same manner specially provided for in this section. No wooden building shall be moved from one lot to another until a sworn petition setting forth the purposes of said removal, and the uses to which said building is to be applied, is filed in the office of the superintendent of buildings, and the written consent of said superintendent is first obtained therefor. No wooden building shall be moved from without to within the fire limits.

§ 34. Every wooden or frame building, with a brick or other front, which may hereafter be damaged to an amount not greater than one-half of the value thereof, exclusive of the value of the foundation thereof, at the time of such damage, may be repaired or rebuilt; but if such damage shall amount to more than one-half of such value thereof, exclusive of the value of the foundation, then such building shall not be repaired or rebuilt, but shall be taken down. The amount and extent of such damage shall be determined upon an examination of the building, by one surveyor who shall be appointed by said superintendent of buildings, and one surveyor who shall be appointed by the owner or owners of said premises. In case these two surveyors do not agree, they shall appoint a third surveyor to take part in such examination, and a decision of a majority of them, reduced to writing and sworn to, shall be conclusive, and such building shall in no manner be repaired or rebuilt until after such decision shall have been rendered. If the damage be by fire, or lightning, or wind storm, and such damage is insured against, then the third surveyor provided for in this section shall be appointed by the Underwriters Association of New York State.

§ 35. No frame dwelling-house hereafter erected shall be occupied by more than one family on each floor nor shall any frame building already erected be altered to be occupied by more than three families. Temporary one-story frame buildings may be erected for the use of builders, within the limits of lots whereon buildings are in the course of erection, or on adjoining vacant lots upon permits issued by the superintendent of buildings. Fences of wood shall not be erected over ten feet high. Signs of wood shall not be erected over two feet high on any building. Piazzas or balconies of wood which do not exceed eight feet in width, and which do not exceed more than three feet above the second story floor beams, may be erected upon the front or side of any detached dwelling-house occupied by not more than two families. In connected houses such piazzas or balconies may be built, provided the same are open on the front and have brick ends not less than eight inches thick, carried up above the roof of such piazza or balcony and coped. The roof of all piazzas, except those of wooden buildings, shall be covered with some fire-proof material. Sheds of wood not over fifteen feet high, open on at least one side, with the sides and roof thereof covered with fire-proof material, may also be built, but no fence shall be used as the back or side of any such shed. Any bay or oriel window that does not extend more than three feet above the second story ceiling line of any dwelling-house may be built of wood. Exterior privies and wood or coal houses, not exceeding one hundred and fifty square feet in superficial area and eight feet high, may be built of wood, but the roofs thereof must be covered with metal, gravel or slate. Sheds erected on piers, wharves or bulkheads on a water front, not exceeding twenty-five feet in height, shall be covered on the outside with slate, tile, metal or other incombustible material. Coal elevators or pockets for the storage of coal and trestle work in connection therewith shall be in mode of construction and location as may be approved by the superintendent of buildings. Grain elevators may be constructed of wood, but all the external wood work shall be covered with incombustible material, and when such building exceeds sixty feet in height, the two lower stories shall be of brick. Lumber or other wood, or second-hand combustible material, shall not be piled at any lesser distance from the nearest dwelling-house than double the height of such pile.

§ 36. Outside of the fire limits before prescribed herein, buildings of frame or wood may be erected, but no frame building, to be occupied or used as a stable, workshop or manufactory, shall be built more than two stories or twenty-five feet in height, nor shall any wooden tower or spire be built or rebuilt to a greater height than sixty feet. No frame or wooden dwelling-house hereafter erected shall exceed three stories or thirty-five feet in height. In no case shall a wooden building be erected within three feet of the side or rear line of a lot, unless the space between the studs on any such side be filled in solidly with not less than four inches of brick work. When two or more such houses are built continuous, the party or division studding shall be not less than four inches thick and filled in solidly with brick work, or the division walls may be of brick not less than eight inches thick above the foundation wall; and the ends of the floor beams shall be so separated that four inches of brick will be between the beams where they rest on said walls. All frame or wooden buildings exceeding a height of fifteen feet shall be built with sills, posts, girts, plates and rafters, all of suitable size and properly mortised, tenoned, braced and pinned, and with suitable studs set at proper distances apart. The floor beams shall not be less than two inches in thickness. The covering of roofs may be of shingle. The sills of wooden dwelling-houses shall be not less than two feet above the ground to the underside of same. All cellar or basement walls of frame or wooden buildings shall be not less than eight inches thick, if of brick, or of a greater thickness if of stone. When any said wall is eight feet or more above the surface of the ground, then the wall shall be not less than twelve inches thick, if of brick, or not less than sixteen inches thick if of stone. Frame buildings sheathed with boards and partially or entirely covered with four inches of brick work shall be deemed to be frame buildings.

§ 37. Every dwelling house occupied by or built to be occupied by three or more families above the first story, and every building already erected, or that may hereafter be erected, more than three stories in height, occupied and used as a hotel or lodging-house, and every boarding-house having more than fifteen sleeping rooms above the basement story, and every factory, mill, manufactory or work-shop, hospital, asylum or institution for the care or treatment of individuals, and every building in whole or in part occupied or used as a school or place of instruction or assembly, and every office building five stories or more in height, shall be provided with such good and sufficient fire-escapes, stairways, or other means of egress in case of fire as shall be directed by the superintendent of buildings. The superintendent of buildings shall make rules and regulations for the construction of outside fire-escape balconies and ladders. Said rules and regulations shall conform to those adopted and published by the Department of Buildings of the City of New York, as such rules and regulations now are or by amendments and additions thereto as may hereafter be prescribed, so far as they may be deemed applicable by the superintendent of buildings in this title named. The superintendent of buildings shall have full and exclusive power and authority within said city to direct fire-escapes and other means of egress to be provided upon and within said building or any of them. The owner or owners of any building upon which a fire-escape is erected shall keep the same in good repair and properly painted. No person shall at any time place any incumbrance of any kind whatsoever before or upon any fire-escape. It shall be the duty of every fireman and policeman who shall discover any fire-escape balcony or ladder of any fire-escape incumbered in any way to forthwith report the same to the commanding officer of his company or precinct, and such commanding officer shall forthwith cause the occupant of the premises or apartment to which said fire-escape balcony or ladder is attached or for whose use the same is provided, to be notified either verbally or in writing, to remove such incumbrance and keep the same clear. If such notice shall not be complied with by the removal, forthwith, of such incumbrance, and keeping said fire-escape balcony or ladder free from incumbrance, then it shall be the duty of said commanding officer, to apply to the nearest magistrate for a warrant for the arrest of the occupant or occupants of the said premises or apartment of which the fire-escape forms a part, and the said parties shall be brought before the said magistrate, as for a misdemeanor; and, on conviction, the occupant or occupants of said premises or apartment shall be fined not more than ten dollars for each offense, or may be imprisoned not to exceed ten days, or both, in the discretion of the court. In constructing all balcony fire-escapes, the manufacturer thereof shall securely fasten thereto in a conspicuous place, a cast-iron plate having suitable raised letters on the same, to read as follows: Notice! Any person placing any incumbrance on this balcony is liable to a penalty of ten dollars and imprisonment for ten days. The owner, proprietor or manager of every hotel and lodging-house, and of every boarding-house having more than fifteen sleeping rooms above the ground floor, and the person or persons having charge or management of every public or private hospital or asylum building, as may be deemed necessary by the chief engineer of the fire department of said city, shall, within three months after the passage of this act, place or cause to be placed in every room used as a lodging or sleeping-room in such building, except the rooms on the ground floor, and also excepting rooms one or more windows of which open upon a fire-escape having direct access to the ground, a manilla rope, or other better appliance to be approved by the said chief of fire department, to be used as an auxiliary means of escape. Said rope or other appliance shall be securely fastened on one end to a suitable iron hook or eye, to be securely driven into or fastened to the wall or stud next adjoining the frame of the window, or one of the windows, of such room, and at all times be coiled up and exposed to the view of the occupant of the room, the coil to be fastened in such slight manner as to be easily and quickly loosened. Said rope shall not be less than one inch in diameter and shall be of sufficient length to reach the ground, and the rope and fastenings shall be of sufficient strength to sustain a weight of not less than one thousand pounds. The chief of said department shall cause any building to which the requirement of rope-escape applies to be periodically inspected to ascertain whether the provisions of this section as to ropes have been complied with, and to report any omission or neglect thereof to the city attorney. The provisions of this section in regard to auxiliary rope fire-escapes shall not apply to fire-proof buildings. All buildings requiring fire-escapes shall have stationary iron ladders leading to the scuttle opening in the roof thereof, and all scuttles and ladders shall be kept so as to be ready for use at all times. If a bulkhead is used in place of a scuttle, it shall have stairs with sufficient guard or hand-rail leading to the roof. In case the building shall be a tenement-house, the door in the bulkhead or any scuttle shall at no time be locked, but may be fastened on the inside by movable bolts or hooks. Every dwelling-house arranged for or occupied by two or more families above the first story, hereafter erected, shall be provided with an entrance to the basement thereof from the outside of such building.

§ 38. The superintendent of buildings shall make rules and regulations in accordance with which the drainage and plumbing of all buildings hereafter erected shall be executed. Said rules and regulations shall conform to those adopted and published by the Department of Buildings of the City of New York, as such rules and regulations now are, or by amendments and additions thereto may hereafter be prescribed, in so far as they may be deemed applicable by the superintendent of buildings in this title named. In each case the owner or his agent, architect or plumber shall file with the superintendent of buildings suitable drawings and descriptions of the drainage and plumbing, and no part of such work shall be commenced or proceeded with until said drawings and descriptions shall have been so filed and approved by the superintendent of buildings.

§ 39. The light and ventilation of every building hereafter erected or altered to be occupied as an apartment-house, tenement-house, lodging-house or hotel shall be provided for in accordance with the rules and regulations to be prescribed by the superintendent of buildings. Said rules and regulations shall conform to those adopted and published by the Department of Buildings of the City of New York, as the said rules and regulations for light and ventilation now are, or by amendments and additions thereto may hereafter be prescribed, so far as they may be deemed applicable by the superintendent of buildings in this title named.

§ 40. In all buildings of a public character, such as hotels, churches, theatres, restaurants, railroad depots public halls and other buildings used or intended to be used for purposes of public assembly, amusement or instruction, the halls, doors, stairways, seats, passageways and aisles, and all lighting and heating appliances and apparatus shall be arranged as the superintendent of buildings shall direct to facilitate egress in cases of fire or accident, and to afford the requisite and proper accommodation for the public protection in such cases. All aisles and passageways in said buildings shall be kept free from camp stools, chairs, sofas and other obstructions, and no person shall be allowed to stand in or occupy any of said aisles or passageways during any performance, service, exhibition, lecture, concert, ball or any public assemblage. The superintendent of buildings, with the concurrence of the chief engineer of the fire department, may, at any time, serve a written or printed notice upon the owner, lessee or manager of any of said buildings, directing any act or thing to be done or provided in or about the said buildings and the several appliances therewith connected, such as halls, doors, stairs, windows, seats, aisles, fire-walls and fire-escapes, so as to afford such security to the public in the uses to which they may be severally applied, as they may deem necessary. Nothing herein contained shall be construed to authorize or require any other alterations to existing theatres than are specified in this section. Upon report to the Mayor of the city, by the superintendent of buildings, that any order or requirement of this title in regard to theatres or places of public amusement has been violated or not complied with, in any such building, the said Mayor may, in his discretion, revoke the license of such theatre or place of public amusement, and cause the same to be closed. No building to be used and occupied as a public school shall hereafter be erected within two hundred feet of a block occupied in whole or in part by a criminal court and prison, or either a criminal court or prison, nor shall it be lawful to hereafter erect a building to be used and occupied as a criminal court and prison, or either of them, within two hundred feet of a block occupied in whole or in part by a public school building.

§ 41. Every theatre or opera house, or other building intended to be used for theatrical or operatic purposes, or for public entertainments of any kind where stage scenery and apparatus are employed, hereafter erected, shall be built to comply with the requirements of this section. No building which, at the time of the passage of this act, is not in actual use for theatrical or operatic purposes, and no building hereafter erected not in conformity with the requirements of this section, shall be used for theatrical or operatic purposes, or for public entertainments of any kind where stage scenery and apparatus are employed, until the same shall have been made to conform to the requirements of this section. And no building hereinbefore described shall be opened to the public for theatrical or operatic purposes, or for public entertainments of any kind where stage scenery or apparatus are employed, until the superintendent of buildings shall have approved the same in writing as conforming to the requirements of this section, and the Mayor of the city shall refuse to issue any license for any such building, and shall close the same, and prevent its opening until a certificate in writing of such approval shall have been given by the superintendent of buildings. Every such building shall have at least one front on the street, and in such front there shall be suitable means of entrance and exit for the audience. In addition to the aforesaid entrances and exits on the street, there shall be reserved for service in case of an emergency, an open court or space on the side not bordering on the street, where said building is located on a corner lot; and on both sides of said building, where there is but one frontage on the street. The width of such open court or courts shall be not less than seven feet where the seating capacity is not over one thousand people, above one thousand and not more than eighteen hundred people, eight feet in width, and above eighteen hundred people, ten feet in width. Said open court or courts shall begin on a line with or near the proscenium wall and shall extend the length of the auditorium proper, to or near the wall separating the same from the entrance lobby or vestibule. A separate and distinct corridor shall continue to the street, from each open court, through such superstructure as may be built on the street side of the auditorium, with continuous walls of brick or fire-proof materials on each side of the entire length of said corridor or corridors, and the ceiling and floors shall be fire-proof. Said corridor or corridors shall not be reduced in width to more than two feet less than the width of the open court or courts, and there shall be no projection in the same; the outer openings to be provided with doors or gates opening toward the street. During the performance the doors or gates in the corridor shall be kept open by proper fastenings; at other times they may be closed and fastened by movable bolts or locks. The said open courts and corridors shall not be used for storage purposes, or for any purpose whatsoever, except for exit and entrance from and to the auditorium and stage, and must be kept free and clear during performances. The level of said corridors at the front entrance to the building shall not be greater than one step above the level of the sidewalk, where they begin at the street entrance, and the entrance of the main front of the building shall not be on a higher level from the sidewalk than four steps, unless approved by the superintendent of buildings. To overcome any difference of level existing between exits from the parquet into courts and the level of the said corridors, gradients shall be employed of not over one foot in ten feet, with no perpendicular risers. From the auditorium opening into the said open courts, or on the side street, there shall be not less than two exits on each side, in each tier, from and including the parquet and each and every gallery. Each exit shall be at least five feet in width in the clear, and provided with doors of iron, or wooden doors covered with tin on both sides and edges. All of said doors shall open outwardly, and must be fastened with movable bolts, the bolts to be kept drawn during performances. There shall be balconies not less than four feet in width in the said open court or courts, at each level or tier above the parquet, on each side of the auditorium, of sufficient length to embrace the two exits, and from said balconies there shall be staircases extending to the ground level, with a rise of not over eight and one-half inches to a step, and not less than nine inches tread exclusive of the nosing. The staircase, from the upper balcony to the next below, shall not be less than thirty inches in width in the clear, and from the first balcony to the ground, three feet in width in the clear, where the seating capacity of the auditorium is one for one thousand people or less, three feet and six inches in the clear where above one thousand and not more than eighteen hundred people, and four feet in the clear where above eighteen hundred people and not more than twenty-five hundred people, and not over four feet six inches in the clear where above twenty-five hundred people. All the before mentioned balconies and staircases shall be constructed of iron throughout, including the floors, and of ample strength to sustain the load to be carried by them, and they shall be covered with a metal hood or awning, to be constructed in such manner as shall be satisfactory to the superintendent of buildings. Where one side of the building borders on a street, there shall be balconies and staircases of like capacity and kind, as before mentioned, but said staircases shall end at a balcony placed not less than seven feet above the level of the ground, and from said balcony to the ground there shall be arranged a hinged iron ladder. When located on a corner lot that portion of the premises bordering on the side street and not required for the uses of the theatre may, if such portion be not more than twenty-five feet in width, be used for offices, stores or apartments, provided the walls separating this portion from the theatre proper are carried up solidly to and through the roof, and that a fireproof exit is provided for the theatre, on each tier, equal to the combined width of exits opening on opposite sides of each tier, communicating with balconies and staircases leading to the street in manner provided elsewhere in this section; said exit passages shall be entirely cut off by brick walls from said offices, stores or apartments and the floors and ceilings in each tier shall be fire-proof. Nothing herein contained shall prevent a roof garden, art gallery, or rooms for similar purposes being placed above a theatre or public building, provided the floor of the same forming the roof over such theatre or building shall be constructed of iron or steel and fireproof materials, and that said floor shall have no covering boards or sleepers of wood, but be of tile or cement. Every roof over said garden or rooms shall have all supports and rafters of iron or steel, and be covered with glass or fire-proof materials, or both, but no such roof garden, art gallery or room for any public purpose shall be placed over or above that portion of any theatre or other building which is used as a stage. No workshop, storage or general property room shall be allowed above the auditorium or stage, or under the same, or in any of the fly galleries. All of said rooms or shops may be located in the rear or at the side of the stage, but in such cases they shall be separated from the stage by a brick wall, and the openings leading into said portions, shall have fire-proof doors on each side of the openings, hung to iron eyes built into the wall. No portion of any building hereafter erected or altered, used or intended to be used, for theatrical or other purposes as in this section specified, shall be occupied or used as a hotel, boarding or lodging-house, factory, workshop or manufactory, or for storage purposes, except as may be hereafter specially provided for. Said restriction relates not only to that portion of the building which contains the auditorium and the stage, but applies also to the entire structure in conjunction therewith. No store or room contained in the building, or the offices, stores or apartments adjoining, as aforesaid, shall be let or used for carrying on any business dealing in articles designated as especially hazardous in the classification of the Underwriters' Association of New York State, or for manufacturing purposes. No lodging accommodation shall be allowed in any part of the building communicating with the auditorium. Interior walls built of fire-proof materials shall separate the auditorium from the entrance vestibule, and from any room or rooms over the same, also from any lobbies, corridors, refreshment or other rooms. All staircases for the use of the audience shall be inclosed with walls of brick, or of fire-proof materials approved by the superintendent of buildings, in the stories through which they pass, and the openings to said staircases from each tier shall be the full width of such staircase. A fire-wall, built of brick, shall separate the auditorium from the stage, and the same shall extend at least four feet above the stage roof, or the auditorium roof, if the latter be the higher, and shall be coped. Above the proscenium opening there shall be an iron girder of sufficient strength to safely support the brick wall above, and covered with fire-proof materials to protect it from the heat. Should there be constructed an orchestra over the stage, above the proscenium opening, the said orchestra shall be placed on the auditorium side of the proscenium fire-wall, and shall be entered only from the auditorium side of the wall. The molded frame around the proscenium opening shall be formed entirely of fire-proof materials; if metal be used, the metal shall be filled in solid with non-combustible material and securely anchored to the wall with iron. The proscenium opening shall be provided with a fire-proof metal curtain, or a curtain of asbestos, or other fire-proof material approved by the superintendent of buildings, sliding at each end within iron grooves or other approved device, securely fastened to the brick wall, and extending beyond the opening not less than six inches on each side. Said fire-proof curtain shall be raised at the commencement of each performance and lowered at the close of said performance, and be operated by approved machinery for that purpose. The proscenium curtains shall be placed at least three feet distant from the foot-lights at the nearest point. All doorways or openings through the proscenium wall, from the auditorium, in every tier, shall have doors of iron, or tin-covered wooden doors, on each face of the wall, and the doors hung so as to be opened from either side at all times. There shall be no openings in the proscenium fire wall above the level of the auditorium ceiling. Direct access to these doors shall be provided on both sides, and the same shall always be kept free from any incumbrance. Iron ladders or stairs, securely fixed to the wall, on the stage side, shall be provided to overcome any difference of level existing between the floor or galleries on the stage side of the fire wall and those on the side of the auditorium. There shall be provided over the stage, metal skylights, of an area or combined area of at least one-twelfth the area of said stage fitted up with sliding sash and glazed with double-thick sheet glass, not exceeding one-eighth of an inch thick, and each pane thereof measuring not less than three hundred square inches, and the whole of which skylight shall be so constructed as to open instantly on the cutting or burning of a hempen cord, which shall be arranged to hold said skylights closed, or some other equally simple approved device for opening them may be provided. Immediately under the glass of said skylights there shall be a wire netting, uuless the glass contains a wire netting within itself. All that portion of the stage not comprised in the work of scenery, traps and other mechanical apparatus, for the presentation of a scene, usually equal to the width of the proscenium opening, shall be built of iron or steel beams filled in between with fire-proof material, and all girders for the support of said beams shall be of wrought-iron or rolled steel. The fly galleries entire, including pin-rails, shall be constructed of iron or steel, and the floors of said galleries shall be composed of iron or steel beams, filled with fire-proof materials, and no wood boards or sleepers shall be used as covering over beams, but the said floors shall be entirely fire-proof. The rigging loft shall be fire-proof, except the floor covering the same. All stage scenery, curtains and decorations made of combustible material, and all wood work on or about the stage, shall be painted or saturated with some non-combustible material to render the same safe against fire, and the finishing coats of paint applied to all wood work throughout the entire building shall be of such kind as will resist fire to the satisfaction of the superintendent of buildings. The roof over the auditorium and the entire main floor of the auditorium and vestibule, also the entire floor of the second story of the front super-structure over the entrance, lobby and corridors, and all galleries and sup-ports for same in the auditorium shall be constructed of iron or steel and fire-proof materials, not excluding the use of wood floor boards and necessary sleepers to fasten the same to, but such sleepers shall not mean timbers of support and the space between the sleepers shall be solidly filled with fire-proof materials. The fronts of each gallery shall be formed of fire-proof materials, excepting the capping, which may be made of wood. The ceiling under each gallery shall be entirely formed of fire-proof materials. The ceiling of the auditorium shall be formed of fire-proof materials. All lathing, wherever used, shall be of wire or sheet metal. The partitions in that portion of the building which contains the auditorium, the entrance vestibule and every room and passage devoted to the use of the audience, shall be constructed of fire-proof materials, including the furring of outside or other walls. None of the walls or ceilings shall be covered with wood sheathing, canvas, or any combustible materials, but this shall not exclude the use of wood wainscoting to a height not to exceed six feet, which shall be filled in solid between the wainscoting and the wall with fire-proof materials. The walls separating the actors' dressing-room from the stage, and the partitions dividing the dressing-rooms, together with the partitions of every passageway from the same to the stage, and all other partitions on or about the stage shall be constructed of fire-proof material approved by the superintendent of buildings. All doors in any of said partitions shall be of iron or of wood covered with tin. All the shelving and cupboards in each and every dressing-room, property-room or other storage rooms, shall be constructed of metal, slate or some fire-proof material. Dressing-rooms may be placed in the fly galleries, provided that proper exits are secured therefrom to the fire-escapes in the open courts, and that the partitions and other matters pertaining to dressing-rooms, shall conform to the requirements herein contained, but the stairs leading to the same shall be fire-proof. All seats in the auditorium, excepting those con-tained in boxes, shall be firmly secured to the floor, and no seat in the auditorium shall have more than six seats intervening between it and an aisle, on either side, and no stool or seat shall be placed in any aisle. All platforms in galleries, formed to receive the seats, shall not be more than twenty-one inches in height of riser, nor less than thirty inches in width of platform. All aisles on the respective floors in the auditorium, having seats on both sides of same, shall be not less than three feet wide where they begin, and shall be increased in width towards the exits, in the ratio of one and one-half inches to five running feet. Aisles having seats on one side only shall be not less than two feet wide at their beginning and increased in width the same as aisles having seats on both sides. The aggregate capacity of the foyers, lobbies, corridors, passages and rooms for the use of the audience, not including aisle space between seats, shall, on each floor or gallery, be sufficient to contain the entire number to be accommodated on said floor or gallery, in the ratio of one hundred and fifty superficial feet of floor room for every one hundred persons. Gradients or inclined planes shall be employed instead of steps, where possible, to overcome slight differences of level in or between aisles, corridors and passages. Every theatre accommodating three hundred persons shall have at least two exits; when accommodating five hundred persons, at least three exits shall be provided, these exits not referring to or including the exits to the open court or courts at the sides of the theatre. Doorways of exit or entrance for the use of the public shall not be less than five feet in width, and for every additional one hundred persons or portions thereof to be accommodated, in excess of five hundred, an aggregate of twenty inches additional exit must be allowed. All doors of exit or entrance shall open outwardly and be hung to swing in such a manner as not to become an obstruction in a passage or corridor, and no such doors shall be closed and locked during any representation, or when the building is open to the public. Distinct and separate places of exit and entrance shall be provided for each gallery above the first. A common place of exit and entrance may serve for the main floor of the auditorium and the first gallery. No passage leading to any stairway communicating with any entrance or exit shall be less than four feet in width in any part thereof. All stairs within the building shall be constructed of fire-proof material throughout. Stairways serving for the exit of fifty people must be at least four feet wide, between railings, or between walls, and for every additional fifty people to be accommodated six inches must be added to their width. In no case shall the risers of any stairs exceed seven and a half inches in height, nor shall the treads, exclusive of nosings, be less than ten and one-half inches wide in straight stairs. No circular or winding stairs for the use of the public shall be permitted. Where the seating capacity is for more than one thousand people, there shall be at least two independent staircases, with direct exterior outlets, provided for each gallery in the auditorium, where there are not more than two galleries, and the same shall be located on opposite sides of said galleries. Where there are more than two galleries, one or more additional staircases shall be provided, the outlets from which shall communicate directly with the principal exit or other exterior outlets. All said staircases shall be of width proportioned to the seating capacity as elsewhere herein prescribed. Where the seating capacity is for one thousand people, or less, two direct lines of staircase only shall be required,.

located on opposite sides of the galleries, and in both cases shall extend from the sidewalk level to the upper gallery, with outlets from each gallery to each of said staircases. At least two independent staircases, with direct exterior outlets, shall also be provided for the service of the stage and shall be located on the opposite sides of the same. All inside stairways leading to the upper galleries of the auditorium shall be inclosed on both sides with walls of fire-proof materials. Stairs leading to the first or lower gallery may be left open on one side, in which case they must be constructed as herein provided for similar stairs leading from the entrance hall to the main floor of the auditorium. But in no case shall stairs leading to any gallery be left open on both sides. When stairs return directly on themselves, a landing of the full width of both flights, without any steps, shall be provided. The outer line of landings shall be curved, so as to avoid square angles. Stairs turning at an angle shall have a proper landing without winders introduced at said turn. In stairs, when two side flights connect with one main flight, no winders shall be introduced and the width of the main flight shall be at least equal to the aggregate width of the side flights. All inclosed staircases shall have, on both sides, strong hand-rails, firmly secured to the wall about three inches distant therefrom and about three feet above the stairs, but said hand-rails shall not run on level platforms and landings where the same is more in length than the width of the stairs. All staircases seven feet and over in width shall be provided with a center hand-rail of hard wood, or metal, not less than two inches in diameter, placed at a height of about three feet above the center of the treads, and supported on wrought-iron or brass standards of sufficient strength, placed not nearer than four feet nor more than six feet apart and securely bolted to the treads or risers of stairs, or both. Every steam boiler which may be required for heating or other purposes shall be located outside of the building, and the space allotted to the same shall be inclosed by walls of masonry on all sides, and the ceiling of such space shall be constructed of fire-proof materials. All doorways in said walls shall have iron doors. No coil or radiator shall be placed in any aisle or passageway used as an exit; but all said coils and radiators shall be placed in recesses formed in the wall or partition to receive the same. All supply, return or exhaust pipes shall be properly incased and protected where passing through floors or near wood work. Stand pipes of two and one-half inches diameter shall be provided, with hose attachments on every floor and gallery, as follows, namely: One on each side of the auditorium in each tier; also one on each side of the stage in each tier, and at least one in the property-room and one in the carpenter's shop, if the same be contiguous to the building. All such stand pipes shall be kept clear from obstruction. Such stand pipes shall be separate and distinct, receiving their supply of water direct from the steam pumps, and shall be fitted with the regulation couplings of the fire department, and shall be kept constantly filled with water by means of an automatic steam pump or pumps, of sufficient capacity to supply all the lines of hose when operated simultaneously; and said pump or pumps shall be supplied with water from the street main and be ready for immediate use at all times during a performance in said building. A separate and distinct system of automatic sprinklers, with fusible plugs, approved by the superintendent of buildings, supplied with water from a tank located on the roof, over the stage, and not connected in any manner with the stand pipes, shall be placed on the ceiling or roof, over the stage, at such intervals as will protect every square foot of stage surface when said sprinklers are in operation. Automatic sprinklers shall also be placed in the dressing-rooms, under the stage, in the carpenter-shop, paint-rooms, store-rooms and property-rooms. A proper and sufficient quantity of two and one-half inch hose, not less than fifty feet in length, fitted with the regulation couplings of the fire-department, and with nozzles attached thereto, and with hose spanners at each outlet, shall be kept always attached to each hose attachment. There shall also be kept in readiness, for immediate use on the stage, at least four casks full of water, and two buckets to each cask. Said casks and buckets shall be painted red. There shall also be provided hand pumps, or other portable fire extinguishing apparatus, and at least four axes, and two twenty-five feet hooks, two fifteen feet hooks and two ten feet hooks on each tier or floor of the stage. Every portion of the building devoted to the uses or accom-modation of the public, also all outlets leading to the streets, and including the open courts and corridors, shall be well and properly lighted during every performance, and the same shall remain lighted until the entire audience has left the premises. At least two or more oil lamps on each side of the auditorium, in each tier, shall be provided on fixed brackets, not less than seven feet above the floor. Said lamps shall be filled with whale or lard oil, and shall be kept lighted during each performance, or in place of said lamps, candles shall be provided. All gas or electric lights in the halls, corridors, lobby, or any other part of said building used by the audience, except the auditorium, must be controlled by a separate shut-off, located in the lobby, and controlled only in that particular place. Gas mains supplying the building shall have independent connections for the auditorium and the stage, and provision shall be made for shutting off the gas from the outside of the building. When interior gas-lights are not lighted by electricity, other suitable appliances, to be approved by the superin-tendent of buildings, shall be provided. All suspended or bracket lights surrounded by glass, in the auditorium, or in any part of the building devoted to the public shall be provided with proper wire netting under-neath. No gas or electric light shall be inserted in the walls, woodwork, ceilings, or in any part of the building unless protected by fire-proof materials. All lights in passages and corridors in said buildings, and wherever deemed necessary by the superintendent of buildings, shall be protected with proper wire net-work. The foot-lights in addition to the wire net-work shall be protected by a strong wire guard or chain placed not less than two feet distant from said foot-lights, and the trough containing said foot-lights shall be formed of and surrounded by fire-proof materials. All border lights shall be constructed according to the best known methods, subject to the approval of the superintendent of buildings, and shall be suspended for ten feet by wire rope. All ducts or shafts used for conducting heated air from the main chandelier, or from any other light or lights, shall be constructed of metal and made double, with an air space between. All stage lights shall have strong metal wire guards or screens, not less than ten inches in diameter, so constructed that any material in contact therewith shall be out of reach of the flames of said stage lights, and shall be soldered to the fixture in all cases. The stand-pipes, gas-pipes, electric wires, hose, and all apparatus for the extinguishing of fire or guarding against the same, as in this section specified shall be in charge and under control of the fire department, and the commissioners of said department are hereby directed to see that the arrangements in respect thereto are carried out and enforced. A diagram or plan of each tier, gallery or floor, showing distinctly the exits therefrom shall be printed in a legible manner on the programme of the performance. Every exit shall have over the same on the inside the word EXIT painted in legible letters not less than eight inches high.

TITLE II.

RELATING TO CITIES HAVING A POPULATION EXCEEDING THIRTY THOUSAND BUT NOT EXCEEDING SEVENTY-FIVE THOUSAND INHABITANTS.

§ 42. The fire department in each of the cities named in section one of this act, to which title two is to apply, is hereby charged with the enforcement of the provisions of this act, as hereby provided for the survey and inspection of buildings, through a "bureau of buildings," which shall be created in said department within thirty days after this act shall take effect.

§ 43. The chief officer of the bureau of buildings hereby created shall be called the superintendent of buildings, and he and the inspectors, clerks and employes shall be appointed by the commissioners of the fire department in such numbers and for such terms and at such compensation as they, the said commissioners, may determine and fix, and shall be subject to removal after written charges shall have been preferred against them and they shall have had an opportunity to be heard thereon. The said bureau shall be furnished, at the expense of the city, with office room, and supplied with furniture, books, blanks, stationery and other supplies as may be necessary for the proper transaction of its business.

§ 44. Sections Nine, Ten, Eleven, Twelve, Thirteen, Fourteen, Fifteen, Sixteen, Seventeen, Eighteen, Nineteen, Twenty, Twenty-one, Twenty-two, Twenty-three, Twenty-four, Twenty-five, Twenty-six, Twenty-seven, Twenty-eight, Twenty-nine, Thirty, Thirty-one, Thirty-two, Thirty-three, Thirty-four, Thirty-five, Thirty-six, Thirty-seven, Thirty-eight, Thirty-nine and Forty of Title One of this Act shall also be deemed to be parts of, and shall apply to the construction, regulation, survey and inspection of buildings within the cities affected by this Title.

§ 45. Every theatre or opera house, or other building intended to be used for theatrical or operatic purposes, or for public entertainments of any kind where stage scenery and apparatus are employed, hereafter erected, shall be built to comply with the requirements of this section. No building which, at the time of the passage of this act, is not in actual use for theatrical or operatic purposes, and no building hereafter erected not in conformity with the requirements of this section, shall be used for theatrical or operatic purposes, or for public entertainments of any kind where stage scenery and apparatus are employed, until the same shall have been made to conform to the requirements of this section. And no building hereinbefore described shall be opened to the public for theatrical or operatic purposes, or for public entertainments of any kind where stage scenery or apparatus are employed, until the superintendent of buildings shall have approved the same in writing as conforming to the requirements of this section, and the Mayor of the city shall refuse to issue any license for any such building, and shall close the same, and prevent its opening until a certificate in writing of such approval shall have been given by the superintendent of buildings. Every such building shall have from and to the street suitable means of entrance and exit for the audience. In addition to the aforesaid entrances and exits on the street, there shall be reserved for service in case of an emergency, an open court or space on the side not bordering on the street, where said building is located on a corner lot; and on both sides of said building, where there is but one frontage on the street. The width of such open court or courts shall be not less than seven feet where the seating capacity is not over one thousand people, above one thousand and not more than eighteen hundred people, eight feet in width, and above eighteen hundred people, ten feet in width. Said open court or courts shall begin on a line with or near the proscenium wall and shall extend the length of the auditorium proper, to or near the wall separating the same from the entrance lobby or vestibule. A separate and distinct corridor shall continue to the street, from each open court, through such superstructure as may be built on the street side of the auditorium, with continuous walls of brick or fire-proof materials on each side the entire length of said corridor or corridors, and the ceiling and floors shall be fireproof. Said corridor or corridors shall not be reduced in width to more than two feet less than the width of the open court or courts, and there shall be no projection in the same; the outer openings to be provided with doors or gates opening toward the street. During the performance the doors or gates in the corridor shall be kept open by proper fastenings; at other times they may be closed and fastened by movable bolts or locks. The said open courts and corridors shall not be used for storage purposes, or for any purpose whatsoever except for exit and entrance from and to the auditorium and stage, and must be kept free and clear during performances. The level of said corridors at the front entrance to the building shall not be greater than one step above the level of the sidewalk where they begin at the street entrance, and the entrance of the main front of the building shall not be on a higher level from the sidewalk than four steps, unless approved by the superintendent of buildings. To overcome any difference of level existing between exit from the parquet into courts and the level of the said corridors, gradients shall be employed of not over one foot in ten feet with no perpendicular risers. From the auditorium opening into the said open courts, or on the side street, there shall be not less than two exits on each side in each tier from and including the parquet and each and every gallery. Each exit shall be at least five feet in width in the clear, and provided with doors of iron, or wooden doors covered with tin on both sides and edges.

All of said doors shall open outwardly, and must be fastened with movable bolts, the bolts to be kept drawn during performances. There shall be balconies not less than four feet in width in the said open court or courts, at each level or tier above the parquet, on each side of the auditorium, of sufficient length to embrace the two exits, and from said balconies there shall be staircases extending to the ground level, with a rise of not over eight and one-half inches to a step, and not less than nine inches tread, exclusive of the nosing. The staircase, from the upper balcony to the next below, shall not be less than thirty inches in width in the clear, and from the first balcony to the ground, three feet in width in the clear where the seating capacity of the auditorium is for one thousand people or less; three feet and six inches in the clear where above one thousand and not more than eighteen hundred people, and four feet in the clear where above eighteen hundred people and not more than twenty-five hundred people, and not over four feet six inches in the clear where above twenty-five hundred people. All the before mentioned balconies and staircases shall be constructed of iron throughout, including the floors, and of ample strength to sustain the load to be carried by them, and they shall be covered with a metal hood or awning, to be constructed in such manner as shall be satisfactory to the superintendent of buildings. Where one side of the building borders on a street there shall be balconies and staircases of like capacity and kind as before mentioned, but said staircases shall end at a balcony placed not less than seven feet above the level of the ground, and from said balcony to the ground there shall be arranged a hinged iron ladder. When located on a corner lot, that portion of the premises bordering on the side street, and not required for the uses of the theatre, may, if such portion be not more than twenty-five feet in width, be used for offices, stores or apartments, provided the walls separating this portion from the theatre proper are carried up solidly to and through the roof, and that a fire-proof exit is provided for the theatre, on each pier, equal to the combined width of exits opening on opposite sides in each tier, communicating with balconies and staircases leading to the street in manner provided elsewhere in this section; said exit passages shall be entirely cut off by brick walls from said offices, stores or apartments and the floors and ceilings in each tier shall be fire-proof. Nothing herein contained shall prevent a roof garden, art gallery, or rooms for similar purposes being placed above a theatre or public building, provided the floor of the same forming the roof over such theatre or building shall be constructed of iron or steel and fire-proof materials, and that said floor shall have no covering boards or sleepers of wood, but be of tile or cement. Every roof over said garden or rooms shall have all supports and rafters of iron or steel, and be covered with glass or fire-proof materials or both, but no such roof garden, art gallery or room for any public purpose shall be placed over or above that portion of any theatre or other building which is used as a stage. No workshop, storage or general property-room shall be allowed above the auditorium or stage, or under the same, or in any of the fly galleries. All of said rooms or shops may be located in the rear or at the side of the stage, but in such cases they shall be separated from the stage by a brick wall, and the openings leading into said portions shall have fire-proof doors on each side of the openings, hung to iron eyes built into the wall. No portion of any building hereafter erected or altered, used or intended to be used for theatrical or other purposes as in this section specified, shall be occupied or used as a hotel, boarding or lodging-house, factory, workshop or manufactory or for storage purposes, except as may be hereafter specially provided for. No store or room contained in the building, or the offices, stores or apartments adjoining, as aforesaid, shall be let or used for carrying on any business dealing in articles designated as especially hazardous in the classification of the Underwriters' Association of New York State, or for manufacturing purposes. No lodging accommodation shall be allowed in any part of the building communicating with the auditorium. Interior walls built of fire-proof materials shall separate the auditorium from the entrance vestibule, and from any room or rooms over the same; also from any lobbies, corridors, refreshment or other rooms. All staircases for the use of the audience shall be inclosed with walls of brick, or fire-proof materials approved by the superintendent of buildings, in the stories through which they pass, and the openings to said staircases from each tier shall be the full width of such staircase. A fire-wall, built of brick, shall separate the auditorium from the stage, and the same shall extend at least four feet above the stage roof, or the auditorium roof, if the latter be the higher, and shall be coped. Above the proscenium opening, there shall be an iron girder of sufficient strength to support the brick wall above, and covered with fire-proof materials to protect it from the heat. Should there be constructed an orchestra over the stage, above the proscenium opening, the said orchestra shall be placed on the auditorium side of the proscenium fire wall, and shall be entered only from the auditorium side of said wall. The molded frame around the proscenium opening shall be formed entirely of fire-proof materials; if metal be used, the metal shall be filled in solid with non-combustible material and securely anchored to the wall with iron. The proscenium opening shall be provided with a fire-proof metal curtain, or a curtain of asbestos, or other fire-proof material approved by the superintendent of buildings, sliding at each end within iron grooves or other approved device, securely fastened to the brick wall, and extending beyond the opening, not less than six inches on each side. Said fire-proof curtain shall be raised at the commencement of each performance and lowered at the close of said performance, and be operated by approved machinery for that purpose. The proscenium curtains shall be placed at least three feet distance from the foot-lights at the nearest point. All doorways or openings through the proscenium wall, from the auditorium, in every tier, shall have doors of iron or tin-covered wooden doors on each face of the walls, and the doors hung so as to be opened from either side at all times. There shall be no openings in the proscenium fire-wall above the level of the auditorium ceiling. Direct access to these doors shall be provided on both sides, and the same shall always be kept free from any incumbrance. Iron ladders or stairs, securely fixed to the wall, on the stage side, shall be provided to overcome any difference of level existing between the floor or galleries on the stage side of the fire-wall and those on the side of the auditorium. There shall be provided over the stage, metal skylights of an area or combined area of at least one-twelfth the area of said stage fitted up with sliding sash and glazed with double-thick sheet glass, not exceeding one-eighth of an inch thick, and each pane thereof measuring not less than three hundred square inches, and the whole of which skylight shall be so constructed as to open instantly on the cutting or burning of a hempen cord, which shall be arranged to hold said skylights closed, or some other simple approved device for opening them may be provided. Immediately under the glass of said skylights there shall be a wire netting, unless the glass contains a wire netting within itself. All that portion of the stage not comprised in the working of scenery, traps and other mechanical apparatus, for the presentation of a scene, usually equal to the width of the proscenium opening shall be built of iron or steel beams filled in between with fire-proof material, and all girders for the support of said beams shall be of wrought-iron or rolled steel. The ceiling or under side of the fly galleries shall be covered with iron or tin over the entire exposed wood work. All stage scenery, curtains and decorations made of combustible material, and all wood work on or about the stage, shall be painted or saturated with some non-combustible material, to render the same safe against fire, to the satisfaction of the superintendent of buildings. Nothing herein contained shall prohibit the use of wood construction for floors not specifically mentioned, roofs and galleries, except that the supports of galleries shall be of iron or steel, provided that all such wood work on or about or under the stage, in the auditorium, all wood furring, the under side of roof boards, the under side of floor boards covering wood construction, fronts of galleries and boxes, shall all be painted or saturated with not less than two coats of some non-combustible material, to render the wood safe against fire, to the satisfaction of the superintendent of buildings. All timber and other wood construction shall be so painted or saturated before being covered in. The finishing coats of paint applied to all wood work throughout the entire building shall be of such kind as will resist fire. The entire main floor of the auditorium and vestibule, also the entire floor of the second story of the front superstructure over the entrance lobby and corridors, shall be constructed of iron or steel and fire-proof materials not including the use of wooden floor boards and necessary sleepers to fasten the same to, but such sleepers shall not mean timbers of support and the space between the sleepers shall be solidly filled with fire-proof materials. The partitions in that portion of the building which contains the auditorium, the entrance vestibule, or any room or passage devoted to the use of the audience, shall be constructed of fire proof materials. None of the walls or ceilings shall be covered with wood sheathing or canvas or any combustible material, but this shall not exclude the use of wood wainscoting to a height not to exceed six feet, which shall be filled in solid between the wainscoting and the wall with fire-proof materials. All lathing, whenever used, shall be of wire or sheet metal. The walls separating the actors' dressing-rooms from the stage, and the partitions dividing the dressing-rooms, together with the partitions of every passage from the same to the stage, and all other partitions on or about the stage, shall be constructed of some fire-proof material approved by the superintendent of buildings. All doors in any of said partitions shall be of iron or of wood covered with tin. All the shelving and cupboards in each and every dressing-room, property-room or other storage-rooms, shall be constructed of metal, slate or some fire-proof material. Dressing-rooms may be placed in the fly-galleries, provided that proper exits are secured therefrom to the fire-escapes in the open courts, and that the partitions and other matters pertaining to dressing-rooms shall conform to the requirements herein contained, but the stairs leading to the same shall be fire-proof. All seats in the auditorium, excepting those contained in boxes, shall be firmly secured to the floor, and no seat in the auditorium shall have more than six seats intervening between it and an aisle, on either side, and no stool or seat shall be placed in any aisle. All platforms in galleries formed to receive the seats shall not be more than twenty-one inches in height of riser, nor less than thirty inches in width of platform. All aisles on the respective floors in the auditorium, having seats on both sides of same, shall be not less than three feet wide where they begin, and shall be increased in width towards the exits in the ratio of one and one-half inches to five running feet. Aisles having seats on one side only shall be not less than two feet wide at their beginning, and increased in width the same as aisles having seats on both sides. The aggregate capacity of the foyers, lobbies, corridors, passages and rooms for the use of the audience, not including aisle space between seats, shall, on each floor or gallery, be sufficient to contain the entire number to be accommodated on said floor or gallery, in the ratio of one hundred and fifty superficial feet or floor room for every one hundred persons. Gradients or inclined planes shall be employed instead of steps, where possible, to overcome slight differences of level in or between aisles, corridors and passages. Every theatre accommodating three hundred persons, shall have, at least, two exits; when accommodating five hundred persons, at least three exits shall be provided, these exits not referring to or including the exits to the open court or courts at the sides of the theatre. Doorways of exit or entrance for the use of the public shall not be less than five feet in width, and for every additional one hundred persons or portions thereof to be accommodated in excess of five hundred, an aggregate of twenty inches additional exit width must be allowed. All doors of exit or entrance shall open outwardly and be hung to swing in such a manner as not to become an obstruction in a passage or corridor, and no such doors shall be closed and locked during any representation, or when the building is open to the public. Distinct and separate places of exit and entrance shall be provided for each gallery above the first. A common place of exit and entrance may serve for the main floor of the auditorium and the first gallery. No passage leading to any stairway communicating with any entrance or exit shall be less than four feet in width in any part thereof. All stairs within the building shall be constructed of fire-proof material throughout. Staircases serving for the exit of fifty people must be at least four feet wide, between railings or between walls, and for every additional fifty people to be accommodated, six inches must be added to their width. In no case shall the risers of any stairs exceed seven and one-half inches in height, nor shall the treads, exclusive of nosings, be less than ten and one-half inches wide in straight stairs. No circular or winding stairs for the use of the public shall be permitted. Where the seating capacity is for more than one thousand people, there shall be at least two independent staircases, with direct exterior outlets, provided for each gallery in the auditorium, where there are not more than two galleries, and the same shall be located on opposite sides of said galleries. Where there are more than two galleries, one or more additional staircases shall be provided, the outlets from which shall communicate directly with the principal exit or other exterior outlets. All staircases shall be of width proportioned to the seating capacity as elsewhere herein prescribed. Where the seating capacity is for one thousand people, or less, two direct lines of staircases only shall be required, located on opposite sides of the galleries, and in both cases shall extend from the sidewalk level to the upper gallery, with outlets from each gallery to each of said staircases. At least two independent staircases, with direct exterior outlets, shall also be provided for the service of the stage and shall be located on the opposite sides of the same. All inside stairways leading to the upper galleries of the auditorium shall be inclosed on both sides with the walls of fire-proof materials. Stairs leading to the first or lower gallery may be left open on one side, in which case they must be constructed as herein provided for similar stairs leading from the entrance hall to the main floor of the auditorium. But in no case shall stairs leading to any gallery be left open on both sides. When stairs return directly on themselves, a landing of the full width of both flights, without any steps, shall be provided, and the outer line of landings shall be curved, so as to avoid square angles. Stairs turning at an angle shall have a proper landing without winders introduced at said turn. In stairs, when two side flights connected with one main flight, no winders shall be introduced, and the width of the main flights shall be at least equal to the aggregate width of the side flights. All inclosed staircases shall have on both sides, strong handrails firmly secured to the wall about three inches distant therefrom and about three feet above the stairs, but said handrails shall not run on level platforms and landings where the same is more in length than the width of the stairs. All staircases seven feet and over in width shall be provided with a center handrail of hard wood, or metal, not less than two inches in diameter, placed at a height of about three feet above the center of the treads and supported on wrought-iron or brass standards of sufficient strength, placed not nearer than four feet nor more than six feet apart, and securely bolted to the treads or risers of stairs or both. Every steam boiler which may be required for heating or other purposes shall be located outside of the building, and the space allotted to the same shall be inclosed by walls of masonry on all sides, and the ceiling of such space shall be constructed of fire-proof materials. All doorways in said walls shall have iron doors. No coil or radiator shall be placed in any aisle or passageway used as an exit but all said coils and radiators shall be placed in recesses formed in the wall or partition to receive the same. All supply, return or exhaust pipes shall be properly incased and protected where passing through floors or near wood work. Stand pipes of two and one-half inches diameter shall be provided with hose attachments on every floor and gallery, as follows, namely: One on each side of the auditorium in each tier; also one on each side of the stage in each tier, and at least one in the property-room and one in the carpenter's shop, if the same be contiguous to the building. All such stand pipes shall be kept clear from obstruction. Such stand pipes shall be separate and distinct, receiving their supply of water direct from the steam pumps and shall be fitted with the regulation couplings of the fire department and shall be kept constantly filled with water by means of an automatic steam pump or pumps, of sufficient capacity to supply all the lines of hose when operated simultaneously; and said pump or pumps shall be supplied with water from the street main and be ready for immediate use at all times during a performance in said building. A separate and distinct system of automatic sprinklers, with fusible plugs approved by the superintendent of buildings, supplied with water from a tank located on the roof over the stage and not connected in any manner with the stand pipes, shall be placed on the ceiling or roof over the stage at such intervals as will protect every square foot of stage surface when said sprinklers are in operation. Automatic sprinklers shall also be placed in the dressing-rooms under the stage, in the carpenter shop, paint-rooms, store-rooms, and property-rooms. A proper and sufficient quantity of two and one-half inch hose, not less than fifty feet in length, fitted with the regulation couplings of the fire department and with nozzles attached thereto, and with hose spanners at each outlet, shall be kept always attached to each hose attachment. There shall also be kept in readiness for immediate use on the stage, at least four casks full of water, and two buckets to each cask. Said casks and buckets shall be painted red. There shall also be provided hand pumps, or other portable fire extinguishing apparatus, and at least four axes, and two twenty-five feet hooks, two fifteen feet hooks and two ten feet hooks on each tier or floor of the stage. Every portion of the building devoted to the uses or accomoda-tion of the public, also all outlets leading to the streets, and including the open courts and corridors, shall be well and properly lighted during every performance, and the same shall remain lighted until the entire audience has left the premises. At least two or more oil lamps on each side of the auditorium, in each tier, shall be provided on fixed brackets, not less than seven feet above the floor. Said lamps shall be filled with whale or lard oil, and shall be kept lighted during each performance, or in place of said lamps candles shall be provided. All gas or electric lights in the halls, corridors, lobby, or any other part of said buildings used by the audience, except the auditorium, must be controlled by a separate shut-off, located in the lobby, and controlled only in that particular place. Gas mains supply-ing the building shall have independent connections for the auditorium and stage, and provision shall be made for shutting off the gas from the outside of the building. When interior gas lights are not lighted by electricity, other suitable appliances, to be approved by the superintendent of build-ings, shall be provided. All suspended or bracket lights, surrounded by glass, in the auditorium, or in any part of the building devoted to the public, shall be provided with proper wire netting underneath. No gas or electric light shall be inserted in the walls, wood-work, ceilings, or in any part of the buildings unless protected by fire-proof materials. All lights in passages and corridors in said buildings, and wherever deemed necessary by the superintendent of buildings shall be protected with proper wire net-work. The foot-lights, in addition to the wire net-work, shall be protected by a strong wire guard or chain placed not less than two feet distant from said foot-lights, and the trough containing said foot-lights shall be formed of and surrounded by fire-proof materials. All border lights shall be constructed according to the best known methods, subject to approval of the superintendent of buildings, and shall be suspended for ten feet by wire. All ducts or shafts used for conducting heated air from the main chandelier, or from any other light or lights, shall be constructed of metal and made double, with an air space between. All stage lights shall have strong metal wire guards or screens, not less than ten inches in diameter, so constructed that any material in contact therewith shall be out of reach of the flames of said stage lights, and shall be soldered to the fixture in all cases. The stand-pipes, gas-pipes, electric wires, hose and all apparatus for the extinguishing of fire or guarding against the same, as in this section specified shall be in charge and under control of the fire department, and the commissioners of said department are hereby directed to see that the arrangements in respect thereto are carried out and enforced. A diagram or plan of each tier, gallery or floor, showing distinctly the exits therefrom, shall be printed in a legible manner on the programme of the performance. Every exit shall have over the same on the inside the word EXIT painted in legible letters not less than eight inches high.

TITLE III.

RELATING TO CITIES HAVING A POPULATION LESS THAN THIRTY THOUSAND INHABITANTS.

§ 46. The fire department in each of the cities named in section one of this act, to which title three is to apply, is hereby charged with the enforcement of the provisions of this act, as hereby provided for the survey and inspection of buildings, through a "bureau of buildings," which shall be created in said department within thirty days after this act shall take effect.

§ 47. The chief officer of the bureau of buildings hereby created shall be called the superintendent of buildings, and he and the inspectors, clerks and employees shall be appointed by the commissioners of the fire department in such numbers and for such terms and at such compensation as they, the said commissioners, may determine and fix, and shall be subject to removal after written charges shall have been preferred against them and they shall have had an opportunity to be heard thereon. The said bureau shall be furnished, at the expense of the city, with office room, and supplied with furniture, books, blanks, stationery and other supplies as may be necessary for the proper transaction of its business.

§ 48. Sections Nine, Ten, Eleven, Twelve, Thirteen, Fourteen, Fifteen, Sixteen, Seventeen, Eighteen, Nineteen, Twenty, Twenty-one, Twenty-two, Twenty-three, Twenty-four, Twenty-five, Twenty-six, Twenty-seven, Twenty-eight, Twenty-nine, Thirty, Thirty-one, Thirty-two, Thirty-three, Thirty-four, Thirty-five, Thirty-six, Thirty-seven, Thirty-eight, Thirty-nine and Forty of Title One of this Act shall also be deemed to be parts of, and shall apply to the construction, regulation, survey and inspection of buildings within the cities affected by this Title.

§ 49. Every theatre or opera house, or other building intended to be used for theatrical or operatic purposes, or for public entertainments of any kind where stage scenery and apparatus are employed, hereafter erected, shall be built to comply with the requirements of this section. No building which, at the time of the passage of this act, is not in actual use for theatrical purposes, or places of amusement, and no building hereafter erected not in conformity with the requirements of this section, shall be used for theatrical or amusement purposes, or for public entertainments of any kind where the stage scenery and apparatus are employed, until the same shall have been made to conform to the requirements of this section. And no building hereinbefore described shall be opened to the public for theatrical purposes, or for public entertainments of any kind where stage scenery or apparatus are employed, until the superintendent of buildings shall have approved the same, in writing, as conforming to the requirements of this section, and the Mayor of the city shall refuse to issue any license for any such building, and shall close the same, and prevent its opening until a certificate in writing of such approval shall have been given by the superintendent of buildings. Every such building shall have suitable means of entrance and exit for the audience. In addition thereto there shall be reserved for service in case of an emergency, an open court or space on the side not bordering on the street, where said building is located on a corner lot; and on both sides of said building, where there is but one frontage on the street. The width of each open court or courts shall not be less than seven feet, and shall begin on a line with or near the proscenium wall, and shall extend the length of the auditorium proper. A separate and distinct corridor shall continue to the street from each open court through such superstructure as may be built on the street side of the auditorium, not less than five feet in width in the narrowest part. Nothing herein contained, however, shall prohibit the use of alleyways, or adjoining premises, where passage may be obtained to the nearest street. Said open courts or corridors shall not be used for storage purposes, or for any purpose whatsoever except for exit and entrance from and to the auditorium and stage, and must be kept free and clear during performances. Such gates or doors as will be provided at street end of said entrances shall be kept open during a performance. The entrance of the main front of the building shall not be on a higher level from the sidewalk than eight steps, unless approved by the superintendent of buildings. To overcome any difference of level existing between exits from the parquet into the courts and the level of the said corridors, gradients shall be employed of not over one foot in ten feet with no perpendicular risers. From the auditorium opening into the said open courts, or on the side street, there shall be not less than two exits on each side in each tier from and including the parquet and each and every gallery. Each exit shall be at least five feet in width in the clear and provided with doors of iron or wooden doors covered with tin on both sides and edges. All of said doors shall open outwardly, and must be fastened with movable bolts, the bolts to be kept drawn during the performance. There shall be balconies not less than four feet in width in the said open courts at each level or tier above the parquet on each side of the auditorium, of sufficient length to embrace the two exits, and from said balconies there shall be staircases extending to the ground level, with a rise of not over eight and one-half inches to a step, and not less than nine inches tread exclusive of the nosing. The staircase from the upper balcony to the next below shall not be less than thirty inches in width in the clear, and from the first balcony

to the ground three feet in width to the clear. All before mentioned balconies and staircases shall be constructed of iron stringers and railings and
hard wood treads and platforms of ample strength to sustain the load to be
carried. Where one side of the building borders on a street there shall be
balconies and staircases of like capacity and kind as before mentioned, but
said staircases shall end at a balcony placed not less than seven feet above the
level of the ground, and from said balcony to the ground there shall be arranged
a hinged iron ladder. When located in the rear of a building bordering on
a street or side street, there shall be a brick wall separating said building or
buildings from the theater proper, and said wall shall be carried up solidly
to the roof. The doors from the theater proper to the exit and entrance
corridors to the street shall be of iron or wood covered with tin. No workshop, storage or general property room shall be allowed above the auditorium
or stage. No store or room contained in the theater proper shall be let or
used for carrying on any business dealing in articles designated as especially
hazardous in the classification of the Underwriters' Association of New York
State, or for manufacturing purposes. A fire-wall, built of brick, shall separate the auditorium from the stage, and the same shall extend at least four
feet above the stage roof and shall be coped. Above the proscenium opening, there shall be an iron girder of sufficient strength to support the brick
wall above, and covered with fire-proof materials to protect it from the heat.
The molded frame around the proscenium opening shall be formed in fire-
proof materials; if metal be used, the metal shall be filled in solid with non-
combustible material and securely anchored to the wall with iron. The proscenium opening shall be provided with a fire-proof curtain of asbestos, or
other fire-proof material approved by the superintendent of buildings. Said
fire-proof curtain shall be raised at the commencement of each performance
and lowered at the close of said performance, and be operated by approved
machinery for that purpose. The proscenium curtain shall be placed at
least three feet distant from the foot-lights at the nearest point. All doorways or openings through the proscenium wall, from the auditorium, in every
tier, shall have iron or tin-covered wooden doors on each face of the wall;
direct access to these doors shall be provided on both sides, and the same
shall always be kept free from any incumbrance. There shall be provided
over the stage, skylights of an area or combined area of at least one-twelfth
the area of said stage fitted with sliding sash, and glazed with double-thick
sheet glass, not exceeding one-eighth of an inch thick, and the whole of
which skylight shall be so constructed as to open instantly on the cutting
or burning of a hempen cord, which shall be arranged to hold said skylight
closed, or some other equally simple approved device for opening them may
be provided. Immediately under the glass of said skylights there shall be
a wire netting, unless the glass contains a wire netting within itself. The
walls separating the actors' dressing-rooms, workshop, storage or general
property-rooms from the stage, shall be of brick, and the openings leading
into said portions shall have iron or tin-covered wooden doors. There shall
be a direct exit from the dressing-room portion to the open-courts, and
should dressing-rooms be placed in the fly-galleries, or elsewhere, there
shall be proper exits provided therefrom to the fire-escapes in the open
courts. All seats in the auditorium, excepting those contained in boxes,
shall be firmly secured to the floor, and no seat in the auditorium shall have

more than seven seats intervening between it and an aisle on either side, and no stool or seat shall be placed in any aisle. All platforms in galleries formed to receive seats shall not be more than twenty-one inches in height of riser, nor less than thirty inches in width of platform. All aisles on the respective floors in the auditorium, having seats on both sides of same, shall be not less than three feet wide where they begin, and shall be increased in width towards the exits in the ratio of one and one-half inches to five running feet. Aisles having seats on one side only shall be not less than two feet wide at their beginning and increased in width the same as aisles having seats on both sides. Gradients or inclined planes shall be employed instead of steps, where possible, to overcome slight difference of level in or between aisles, corridors and passages. Every theater accommodating three hundred persons shall have at least two exits; when accommodating five hundred persons, at least three exits shall be provided; these exits not referring to or including the exits to the open court or courts at the side of the theater. Doorways of exit or entrance for the use of the public shall not be less than five feet in width, and for every additional one hundred persons or portion thereof to be accommodated in excess of five hundred an aggregate of twenty inches additional exit width must be allowed. All doors of exit or entrance shall open outwardly and be hung to swing in such manner as not to become an obstruction in a passage or corridor, and no such doors shall be closed and locked during any representation or when the building is open to the public. A common place of exit and extrance may serve for the main floor of the auditorium and the first gallery. There shall be at least two independent staircases leading to the upper gallery located on opposite sides with outlets from each gallery to each of said staircases. Stairways serving for the exit of fifty people must be at least four feet wide, and for every additional fifty people to be accommodated six inches must be added to every width. In no case shall the risers in stairs exceed seven and one-half inches in height, nor shall the treads exclusive of nosing be less than ten and one-half inches wide in straight stairs. No circular or winding stairs for the use of the public shall be permitted. All such staircases shall connect directly with the common place of exit and entrance or other exterior outlets. When stairs return directly on themselves, a landing of the full width of both flights, without any steps, shall be provided. Stairs turning at an angle shall have a proper landing without winders introduced at said turn. In stairs, when two side flights connect with one main flight, no winders shall be introduced. All staircases shall have on both sides strong hand-railings, and where inclosed shall have on both sides strong hand-rails firmly secured to the wall, about three inches distant therefrom and about three feet above the stairs. Nothing herein contained shall prohibit the use of wood construction for floors, roofs, galleries, except that the supports of galleries shall be of iron or steel, stairways and partitions not specifically mentioned, provided that all such wood-work, including the wood-work on or about or under the stage, all wood, furring studding, back of lathing, underside of stage, all wood, furring studding, back of lathing, underside of floor and roof-boards, timbers, stair stringers, back of treads and risers, and wainscoting fronts of galleries and boxes shall be painted or saturated with not less than two coats of some non-combustible material, to render the wood safe against fire, to the satisfaction of the superintendent of buildings. All timber and other wood construction shall be so painted or saturated before being covered in. The finishing coats of paint applied to all wood-work throughout the entire building shall be of such kind as will resist fire. Every portion of the building devoted to the uses or accommodation of the public, also all outlets leading to the street, shall be well and properly lighted during every performance, and the same shall remain lighted until the entire audience has left the premises. Gas and electrical mains supplying any theater shall have independent connections for the auditorium and the stage, and provision shall be made for shutting off said mains from the outside. All ducts or shafts used for conducting heated air from over the main chandelier, and from any other light or lights, shall be constructed of metal and made double, with an air space between. Where interior gas lights are not lighted by electricity, suitable appliances, approved by the superintendent of buildings, shall be provided. All stage lights shall have strong metal wire guards or screens, not less than ten inches in diameter, so constructed that any material in contact therewith shall be out of reach of the flames of said stage lights, and shall be soldered to the fixtures in all cases. All border lights shall be constructed according to the best known methods, subject to the approval of the superintendent of buildings, and shall be suspended for ten feet by wire rope. The foot-lights shall be protected by wire net-work, and in addition thereto there shall be a strong wire-guard or chain, placed not less than two feet distant from said foot-lights, and the trough containing said foot-lights shall be lined with tin. Every steam-boiler which may be required for heating or other purposes shall be located outside of the theater proper, and the space allotted to the same shall be inclosed by walls of masonry on all sides, and the ceiling of said space shall be constructed of fire-proof materials. All doorways in said walls shall have iron doors. No coil or radiator shall be placed in any aisle or passageway used as an exit; but all said coils and radiators shall be placed in recesses formed in the wall or partitions to receive the same, and the recesses thus formed, if in a wood partition, shall be lined with metal. All supply, return or exhaust pipes shall be properly incased and protected where passing through floors or near wood-work. Stand pipes shall be provided, with hose attachments, as follows: One on each side of the stage in each tier and at least one in the property-room and one in the carpenter's shop, if the same be contiguous to the theater and all kept clear from obstruction. A proper and sufficient quantity of hose not less than fifty feet in length shall be kept always attached to each hose attachment. Said stand pipes shall receive their supply of water direct from the street main, providing that the pressure is sufficient to reach the roof over the stage from the nearest hose attachment. If the pressure of water is insufficient, the stand pipes shall be supplied with water from a tank located on the roof over the stage, the said tank to be supplied with water by means of a steam-pump. There shall also be kept in readiness for immediate use on the stage, buckets of water or portable fire-extinguishing apparatus, and at least four axes on each tier or floor. The stand pipes, gas pipes, electric wires, hose and all apparatus for the extinguishing of fire or guarding against the same, as in this section specified, shall be in charge and under the control of the fire department, and the commissioners of said department are hereby directed to see that the arrangements in respect thereto are carried out and enforced. A diagram or plan of each tier, gallery or floor, showing distinctly the exits therefrom, shall be printed in a legible manner on the programme of the performance. Every exit shall have over the same, on the inside, the word EXIT painted in legible letters not less than eight inches high.

GENERAL PROVISIONS AND REQUIREMENTS.

APPLICABLE TO ALL CITIES COMING WITHIN THE PROVISIONS OF THIS ACT.

§ 50. Before the erection, construction or alteration of any building or part of any building, or any platform, staging or flooring to be used for standing or seating purposes is commenced, the owner, or his agent or architect, shall submit to the superintendent of buildings a full and complete copy of the plans of such proposed work, and a detailed statement, in duplicate, of the specifications, on appropriate blanks to be furnished to applicants by the superintendent of buildings, giving also the location, the proposed use of the building or structure, and the estimated cost of the same, which shall be accompanied with a statement in writing, sworn to before a notary public or commissioner of deeds, giving the full name and residence (street and number) of the owner, or of each of the owners of said building, or proposed building, platform, staging or flooring. If such erection, construction or alteration is proposed to be made by any other person than the owner or owners of the land in fee, the person or persons intending to make such erection or alteration shall accompany said detailed statement of the specifications, and copy of the plans, with a statement in writing, sworn to as aforesaid, giving the full name and residence (street and number) of the owner or owners of the land, and also of every person interested in said building or proposed building, platform, staging or flooring, either as owner, lessee, or in any representative capacity. Such statement may be made by the agent or architect of the person or persons hereinbefore required to make the same, and any notice served upon such agent or architect by the superintendent of buildings shall be binding upon the principals. Said sworn statement, and detailed statement and copy of the plans shall be kept on file in the office of the superintendent of buildings, and the erection, construction or alteration of said building, platform, staging or flooring, or any part thereof, shall not be commenced or proceeded with, until said statement and plans shall have been so filed, and approved by the superintendent of buildings, and a permit issued by him therefor. Any permit so issued, but under which no building work is commenced within one year from the time of issuance, shall expire by limitation. But the superintendent may, in his discretion, and for reasons to be stated in writing, by the applicant, and filed with the plans and detailed statement, dispense with the making of said sworn statement in any case. Nothing in this section shall be construed to prevent the superintendent of buildings from granting his approval for the erection of any part of a building where plans and detailed statements have been presented for the same before the entire plans and detailed statements of said building have been submitted. Any false swearing in a material point in any statement submitted in pursuance of the provisions of this section shall be deemed perjury and shall be punished as such. Ordinary repairs may be made without notice to the superintendent of buildings, but such repairs shall not be construed to include the cutting away of any stone or brick wall, or any portion thereof, the removal or cutting of any beams or supports, or the removal, change or closing of any staircase.

§ 51. The superintendent of buildings shall have power (except as herein otherwise provided) to pass upon any question relative to the mode, manner of construction, or materials to be used, in the erection or alteration of any building, or other structure provided for in this act, to make the same conform to the true intent and meaning of the several provisions of this act. He shall also have power to vary or modify the provisions of this act, upon application to him therefor in writing, by an owner of such building or structure, or his representative, where there are practical difficulties in the way of carrying out the strict letter of this law, so that the spirit of the law shall be observed, the public safety secured and substantial justice done; but no such deviation shall be permitted unless a record of the same shall be kept by the said superintendent of buildings, and a certificate be first issued to the party applying for the same. In cases in which it is claimed by an owner, in person or by his representative, that the provisions of this act do not directly apply, or that an equally good and more desirable form of construction can be employed in any specific case than that required by this act, but a permit for which has been refused by the superintendent of buildings, then such person shall have the right to present a petition to the superintendent of buildings, together with a deposit of thirty dollars, requesting the appointment of an examining board, and thereupon the superintendent of buildings shall appoint a disinterested and competent architect or builder, the applicant shall appoint a second, and the two so chosen shall select a third. The said examiners shall each take the usual oath of office before entering upon the performance of their duties. They shall meet in the office of the superintendent of buildings, and the applicant, or his representative, or both, may appear before said board and be heard. The said board shall consider such petition and, as soon as practicable, render a decision thereon. The said board of examiners are hereby authorized and empowered to grant or reject such petition, and the decision of a majority of them, reduced to writing, and addressed to the superintendent of buildings, shall be final and conclusive. If such decision is favorable to said petitioner, a certificate shall be issued by the superintendent of buildings in accordance therewith. Each of the three examiners shall receive for his services ten dollars from the money deposited with the superintendent of building for that purpose.

§ 52. The owner or owners of any building, or part thereof, upon which any violation of this act may be placed, or shall exist, and any architect, builder, carpenter or mason who may be employed or assist in the commission of any such violation, and any and all persons who shall violate any of the provisions of this act, or fail to comply therewith, or any requirement thereof, or who shall violate, or fail to comply with, any order or regulation made thereunder, or who shall build in violation of any detailed statement of specifications or plans, submitted and approved thereunder, or of any certificate of permit issued thereunder, shall severally, for each and every such violation, or non-compliance, respectively forfeit and pay a penalty in the sum of fifty dollars, except that any such person who shall violate any of the provisions of this act as to the construction of chimneys, fire-places, flues, hot-air pipes and furnaces, or with reference to the framing or trimming of timbers, girders, beams or other wood work proximate to chimney flues or fire-places, shall forfeit and pay a penalty in the sum of one hundred dollars. But if any said violation shall be removed, or be in process of removal, within ten days after the service of a notice as hereinafter prescribed, the liability for such penalty shall cease, and said department of buildings or fire department, as the case may be, shall discontinue any action pending to recover the same, upon such removal, or the completion thereof within a reasonable time. Any and all of the afore-mentioned persons, who having been served with a notice as hereinafter prescribed, to remove any violation, or comply with any requirement of this act, or with any order or regulation made thereunder, shall fail to comply with said notice within ten days after such service, or shall continue to violate any requirement of this act in the respect named in said notice, shall pay a penalty of one hundred dollars. The superintendent of buildings is hereby authorized, in his discretion, good and sufficient cause being shown therefor in writing and filed in his office, to remit any fine or fines, penalty or penalties, and costs which any person or persons may have incurred, under any of the provisions of this act.

§ 53. Superintendents of buildings and deputy superintendents of buildings shall be competent architects or builders of at least ten years' practice. The inspectors shall be competent men, either architects, civil engineers, masons, carpenters or iron workers, who have served at least ten years as such. They shall be men of good character, capable of writing a fair hand, and able to make out with clearness their reports, and no person shall serve as or be appointed to office as an inspector of buildings who is deficient in these qualifications. It shall not be lawful for any officer or employee in any department or bureau of buildings to be engaged in conducting or carrying on business as an architect, civil engineer, carpenter, iron worker, mason or builder. The superintendent of buildings shall be authorized to designate in writing the deputy superintendent of buildings, or any of the inspectors, to act on any survey authorized by this act, or perform such other duties as the said superintendent may direct. The deputy superintendent of buildings or an inspector when there is no deputy, to be designated by the superintendent, shall act as superintendent of buildings in case of absence of the superintendent from his office, and shall while so acting, possess all the powers in this act vested in or imposed upon the superintendent of buildings. The officers, clerks and messengers of the said department or bureau of buildings shall perform such duties as they and each of them may be directed to perform by the superintendent of buildings. Any inspector of buildings for any neglect of duty, or omission to properly perform his duty, or violation of rules, or neglect or disobedience of orders, or incapacity, or absence without leave, may be punished by the superintendent of buildings by forfeiting and withholding pay for a specified time, or by suspension from duty with or without pay; but this provision shall not be deemed to abridge the right to remove or dismiss any such inspector. All the officers appointed under this act, shall, so far as may be necessary for the performance of their respective duties, have the right to enter any building or premises in said city.

§ 54. All suits or proceedings instituted for the enforcement of any of the provisions of this act, or for the recovery of any penalty thereunder, shall be brought in the name of the department of buildings or the fire department, as the case may be, of said city, by the city attorney, to whom all notices of violation shall be returned for prosecution, and it shall be his duty to take charge of the prosecution of all such suits or proceedings, collect and receive all moneys that may be collected upon judgments, suits or proceedings so instituted, or which may be paid by any parties who have violated any of the provisions of this act, and upon settlement of judgment and removal of violations thereunder, execute satisfaction therefor. He shall, quarterly, render to the city treasurer an account of all penalties and all other money, including costs, received by him, together with his bill for all necessary disbursements incurred or paid in said suits, and shall pay over quarterly the amount of such penalties and costs so collected to the city treasurer as a fund for the use and benefit of the said department or bureau of buildings, as the case may be, for the purposes of paying any expense incurred by said department or bureau under Section Sixty-one of this Act, and also for the purpose of carrying into effect any order or precept issued by any court or judge or justice thereof in this act named, to the said department or bureau or superintendent of buildings, and upon the requisition of said department, bureau or superintendent of buildings, said city treasurer shall pay such sum or sums as may be allowed and taxed by any court of record, or a judge or justice thereof, for such purposes, as far as the same may be in his hands. By city attorney, as in this act used, is intended the officer or person who, under existing laws, is authorized to appear for and represent the city, or its municipal departments, as attorney, in legal proceedings in behalf of or against such city or municipal departments. By city treasurer, as in this act used, is intended the chief financial officer of the city, by whatever title designated in existing laws, and by fire commissioners is intended the officers of the fire department performing the duties of fire commissioners.

§ 55. All courts of record, and justices and judges thereof, in the county in which any city may be located, shall have cognizance of and jurisdiction over all suits brought in such city for the recovery of any penalty and of all actions and proceedings, either legal or equitable, that may be appropriate or necessary for the enforcement of the provisions of this act, and are hereby invested with full legal and equitable jurisdiction to hear, try and determine all such actions and proceedings, and to make appropriate orders and render judgment therein according to law, so as to give force and effect to its provisions. Whenever the superintendent of buildings is satisfied that any building or structure, or any portion thereof, the erection, construction, or alteration of which is regulated, permitted or forbidden by this act, is being erected, constructed or altered, or has been erected, constructed or altered, in violation of, or not in compliance with, any of the provisions or requirements of this act, or in violation of any detailed statement of specifications or plans submitted and approved thereunder, or of any certificate of permit issued thereunder, or that any provision or requirement of this act, or any order or direction made thereunder has not been complied with, said city attorney, upon notice from the superintendent of buildings, may institute any appropriate action or proceeding, at law or in equity, to restrain, correct or remove such violation, or to restrain or correct the erection or alteration of, or to require the removal of, or to prevent the occupation or use of the building or structure erected, constructed or altered, in violation of, or not in compliance with any of the provisions of this act, or with respect to which the requirements of this act, or of any order or direction made pursuant to any provisions contained in this act, shall not have been complied with. In any such action or proceeding said city attorney may, on the affidavit of the superintendent of buildings, setting forth the facts, apply to any court of record in said city, or in the county in which said city is situated, or in an adjoining county, or to a judge or justice thereof, for an order enjoining and restraining all persons from doing, or causing or permitting to be done, any work in or upon such building or structure, or in or upon such part thereof, as may be designated in said affidavit, or from occupying or using said building or structure, or such portion thereof as may be designated in said affidavit, for any purpose whatever, until the hearing and determination of said action and the entry of final judgment therein. The court, or judge or justice thereof, to whom such application is made, is hereby authorized forthwith to make any or all of the orders above specified, as may be required in such application, with or without notice, and to make such other or further orders or directions as may be necessary to render the same effectual. No officer of any department or bureau of buildings created under this act, acting in good faith and without malice, shall be liable for damages by reason of anything done in any such action or proceeding. No undertaking shall be required as a condition of the granting or issuing of such injunction order, or by reason thereof All courts in which any suit or proceeding is instituted under this act shall, upon the rendition of a verdict, report of a referee, or decision of a judge or justice, render judgment in accordance therewith; and the said judgment so rendered shall be and become a lien upon the premises named in the complaint in any such action, to date from the time of the filing in the county clerk's office in the county where the property affected by such notice is situated, of a notice of *lis pendens* therein; which lien may be enforced against said property, in every respect, notwithstanding the same may be transferred subsequent to the filing of the said notice. Said notice of *lis pendens* shall consist of a copy of the notice issued by the superintendent of buildings, requiring the removal of the violation and a notice of the suit or proceeding instituted, or to be instituted, thereon, and said notice of *lis pendens* may be filed at any time after the service of the notice issued by the superintendent of buildings as aforesaid. Any notice of *lis pendens* filed pursuant to the provisions of this act may be vacated and discharged of record, upon an order of a judge or justice of the court in which such suit or proceeding was instituted or is pending, or upon the consent in writing of the city attorney, and the clerk in whose office said

notice of *lis pendens* is filed is hereby directed and required to mark any
such notice of *lis pendens*, and any record or docket thereof, as vacated and
discharged of record, upon the presentation and filing of a certified copy of
an order as aforesaid, or of the consent, in writing, of said city attorney. In
no case shall any said department or bureau of buildings, or any officer
thereof, or any defendant, be liable for costs in any action, suit or proceeding that may be instituted or commenced, in pursuance of this act, unless
specially ordered and allowed by a court or justice, in the course of such
action, suit or proceeding. But an execution against the person of the
judgment debtor shall not be issued upon any judgment for a penalty imposed by this act.

§ 56. All notices of the violation of any of the provisions of this act,
and all notices directing anything to be done, required by this act, and all
other notices that may be required or authorized to be issued thereunder,
including notice that any building, structure, premises, or any part thereof,
is deemed unsafe or dangerous, shall be issued by the superintendent of
buildings, and shall have his name affixed thereto, and may be served by
any officer or employee of any department or bureau of buildings, or by any
person authorized by the same. All such notices, and any notice or order
issued by any court in any proceeding instituted to restrain or remove any
violation, or to enforce compliance with any provision or requirement of
this act, may be served by delivering to and leaving a copy of the same,
with any person or persons violating, or who may be liable under any of the
several provisions of this act, or to whom the same may be addressed, and if
such person or persons can not be found after diligent search shall have
been made for him or them, then such notice or order may be served by
posting the same in a conspicuous place upon the premises where such
violation is alleged to have been placed or to exist, or to which such notice
or order may refer, or which may be deemed unsafe or dangerous, which
shall be equivalent to a personal service of said notice or order upon all
parties for whom such search shall have been made. Such notice or order
shall contain a description of the building, premises or property upon
which such violation shall have been put or may exist, or which may be
deemed unsafe or dangerous, or to which such notice or order may refer.
If the person or persons, or any of them, to whom said notice or order is
addressed, do not reside in the State of New York, and have no known
place of business therein, the same may be served by delivering to, and
leaving with, such person or persons, or either of them, a copy of said
notice or order, or if said person or persons can not be found within said
State after diligent search, then by posting a copy of the same in manner as
aforesaid and depositing a copy thereof in the post office of any such city,
inclosed in a sealed wrapper addressed to said person or persons at his or
their last known place of residence, with the postage paid thereon; and
said posting and mailing of a copy of said notice or order shall be equivalent to personal service of said notice or order.

§ 57. Any building or buildings, part or parts of a building, staging
or other structure, that from any cause may now be, or shall at any time
hereafter become dangerous or unsafe, may be taken down and removed, or
made safe and secure, in the manner following: Immediately upon such
unsafe or dangerous building or buildings, or part or parts of a building,

staging or structure being so reported by any of the officers of said department or bureau of buildings, as the case may be, the same shall be immediately entered upon a docket of unsafe buildings, to be kept by said superintendent; and the owner, or some one of the owners, executors, administrators, agents, lessees, or any other person or persons who may have a vested or contingent interest in the same, may be served with a printed or written notice containing a description of the premises or structure and the parts deemed unsafe or dangerous, requiring the same to be made safe and secure, or removed, as the same may be deemed necessary by the said superintendent, which said notice shall require the person or persons thus served to immediately certify to the superintendent of buildings his or their assent or refusal to secure or remove the same.

§ 58. If the person or persons so served with notice shall immediately certify his or their assent to the securing or removal of said unsafe or dangerous building, premises or structure, he or they shall be allowed until one o'clock, p. m., of the day following the service of such notice in which to commence the securing or removal of the same; and he or they shall employ sufficient labor and assistance to secure or remove the same as expeditiously as the same can be done. But upon his or their refusal or neglect to comply with the requirements of said notice so served, a further notice shall be served upon the person or persons heretofore named, and in the manner heretofore prescribed, notifying him or them that a survey of the premises named in said notice will be made at the time and place therein named, which time shall not be less than twenty-four hours nor more than three days from the time of the service of the said notice, by three competent persons, each of whom shall be a practical builder or architect, and one of whom shall be the superintendent of buildings, or an inspector duly authorized by him, or the deputy superintendent of buildings, another of whom shall be appointed by the person or persons thus notified, and the third by the two thus chosen; and that in case the said premises shall be reported unsafe or dangerous by said surveyors, or a majority of them, the said report will be presented to a court of record therein named, which shall be a court held within said city, or within the county in which said city is situated, or in an adjoining county, and that a trial upon the allegations and statements contained in said report, be the report of the said surveyors more or less than is contained in the said notice of survey, will be had before said court, at a time and place therein named, to determine whether said unsafe or dangerous building or premises shall be repaired and secured or taken down and removed; and a report of such survey, reduced to writing, shall constitute the issue to be placed before the court for trial. If the person or persons on whom said notice is served refuse or neglect to appoint a surveyor, within a time fixed in the notice, the superintendent of buildings shall appoint a builder or architect to act for the person or persons so served with notice, and said two persons may make the survey, and in case of disagreement they shall appoint a third person, a builder or architect, to take part in the survey. If the person acting on behalf of any department or bureau of buildings and the surveyor appointed by the person or persons on whom any such notice was served shall neglect or refuse to choose a third person to act upon any survey, within a reasonable time, the superintendent of buildings shall designate such third person. A copy of said report of survey shall be posted on the building, by the persons holding the survey, immediately on their signing the same. The architect or builder appointed by the superintendent of buildings when the person or persons notified neglect or refuse to appoint, as also the architect or builder who may serve as a third surveyor on any survey called in accordance with the provisions of this act, shall each receive the sum of ten dollars, to be paid by the city treasurer upon the voucher of the superintendent of buildings, and a cause of action is hereby created for the benefit of said city against the owner or owners of said building, staging or structure, and of the lot or parcel of land on which the same is situated, for the amount so paid with interest, which shall be prosecuted in the name of the city. The amount so collected shall be paid over to the city treasurer in reimbursement of the amounts paid by him as aforesaid.

§ 59. Whenever the report of any such survey, had as aforesaid, shall recite that the building, premises or structure thus surveyed is unsafe or dangerous, the city attorney shall, at the time in the said notice named, present said notice and report to the judge or justice holding the court in the said notice named, which said judge or justice shall immediately proceed to obtain and impanel a jury, and to the trial of said issue before said jury, giving precedence to the trial of this issue over every other business, and said judge or justice shall have power to impanel a jury for that purpose from any jurors in attendance upon said court, or in case sufficient jurors shall not be in attendance, then from any jurors that may be summoned for that purpose, and said judge or justice shall have power to summon jurors for that purpose; and any such suit or proceedings commenced before a judge or justice may be continued before another judge or justice of the same court; a jury trial may be waived by the default of the defendant or defendants to appear at the time and place named in the said notice, or by agreement, and in such case the trial may be by the court, judge, justice or referee; and upon the rendition of a verdict or decision of the court, judge, justice or referee, if the said verdict or decision shall find the said building, premises or structure to be unsafe or dangerous, the judge or justice trying said cause, or to whom the report of the referee trying said cause shall be presented, shall immediately issue a precept out of said court, directed to the superintendent of buildings, reciting said verdict or decision, and commanding him forthwith to repair and secure, or take down and remove, as the case may be, in accordance with said verdict or decision, said unsafe or dangerous building, buildings, part or parts thereof, staging, structure or other premises that shall have been named in the said report; and said superintendent shall immediately thereupon proceed to execute said precept as therein directed, and may employ such labor and assistance, and furnish such materials as may be necessary for that purpose, and after having done so, said superintendent shall make return of said precept, with an indorsement of his action thereunder, and the cost and expenses thereby incurred, to the said court, and thereupon a judge or justice of said court shall tax and adjust the amount indorsed upon said precept, and shall adjust and allow disbursements of said proceeding, together with the preliminary expenses of searches and surveys, which shall be inserted in the judgment in said action or proceeding, and shall render judgment for such amount, and for the sale of the said premises in the said notice named, together with all the right, title and interest that the person or persons, or either of them, named in the said notice had in the lot, ground or land upon which the said building or structure was placed at the time of the filing of a notice of *lis pendens* in the said proceedings, or at the time of the entry of judgment therein to satisfy the same, which shall be in the same manner and with like effect as sales under judgment in foreclosure of mortgages; and in and about all preliminary proceedings, as well as the carrying into effect any order of the court or any precept issued by any court, said department or bureau of buildings, or fire department, as the case may be, may make requisition upon the city treasurer for such amount or amounts of money as shall be necessary to meet the expenses thereof; and upon the same being approved by any judge or justice of the court from which the said order or precept was issued and presented to said city treasurer, he shall pay the same, and for that purpose shall borrow and raise, upon revenue bonds to be issued in the name of the said city, the several amounts that may from time to time be required, or the city may transfer to the order of the city treasurer, for this purpose, such amounts as may be necessary, from any unexpended or excessive appropriations of the current or any previous year, which shall be reimbursed by the payment of the amount, and interest at six per cent. out of the judgment or judgments obtained as aforesaid, if the same shall be collected. In case said issue shall not be tried at the time specified in said notice, or to which the trial may be adjourned, the same may be brought to trial at any time thereafter without a new survey, upon not less than three days' notice of trial to the person or persons upon whom the original notice was served, or to his or their attorney, which notice of trial may be served in the same manner as said original notice. The notice of *lis pendens* provided for in this section shall consist of a copy of said notice of survey, and shall be filed in the office of the clerk of the county where the premises affected by said notice are situated. Provided nevertheless, that immediately upon the issuing of said precept the owner or owners of said building or premises or any party interested therein, upon application to said superintendent of buildings, shall be allowed to perform the requirements of said precept, at his or their own proper cost and expense, provided the same shall be done immediately, and in accordance with the requirements of said precept, upon the payment of all costs and expenses incurred up to that time.

§ 60. In case any notice or direction authorized to be issued by this act is not complied with within ten days after the service thereof the superintendent of buildings, through the city attorney, may apply to a court of record within said city, or to a judge or justice of a court of record residing or holding court in said city, or to a court of record, or a judge or justice thereof, within the county in which said city is situated, or in an adjoining county, for an order directing the department or bureau of buildings, as the case may be, to proceed to make the alterations or remove the violation or violations, as the same may be specified in said notice or direction. Whenever any notice requires fire-escapes or means of egress in case of fire, to be placed in or upon any building, shall have been served as directed in this act, and the same shall not have been complied with within ten days after service thereof, the superintendent of buildings, through the city attorney, may, in addition to or in lieu of the remedy last above provided, apply to a court of record or to a judge or justice thereof, as last above provided, for an order directing the department or bureau of buildings, as the case may be, to vacate such building or premises, or so much thereof as said department or bureau may deem necessary, and prohibiting the same to be used or occupied for any purpose specified in said order, until such notice shall have been complied with. The expenses and disbursements incurred in the carrying out of any of said orders shall become a lien upon said building or premises named in the said notice, from the time of filing of a copy of the said notice, with a notice of the proceedings taken thereunder, in the office of the clerk of the county within which the premises affected by said notice are situated; and the said court, or a judge or a justice thereof, to whom application shall be made, is hereby authorized and directed to grant any of the orders above named, and to take such proceedings as shall be necessary to make the same effectual, and any such lien may be enforced in the same manner as liens acquired under the mechanics' lien law. In case any of the notices provided for in this act shall be served upon any lessee or party in possession of the building or premises therein described, it shall be the duty of the person upon whom such service is made to give immediate notice to the owner or agent of said building named in the notice, if the same shall be known to the said person personally, if such person shall be within the limits of the city, and his residence known to such person, and if not within said city, then by depositing a copy of said notice in the post-office, properly inclosed and addressed to such owner or agent, at his then place of residence, if known, and by paying the postage thereon. In case any lessee or party in possession shall neglect or refuse to give such notice as herein provided, he shall be personally liable to the owner or owners of said building or premises for all damages he or they shall sustain by reason thereof.

§ 61. In case of the falling of any building or part of any building in any city to which this act relates, where persons are known or believed to be buried under the ruins thereof, it shall be the duty of the fire department to cause an examination of the premises to be made for the recovery of the bodies of the killed and injured. In case there shall be, in the opinion of the superintendent of buildings, actual and immediate danger of the falling of any building or part thereof, so as to endanger life or property, said superintendent shall cause the necessary work to be done to render said building or part thereof temporarily safe, until the proper proceedings can be taken, as in the case of an unsafe building, as provided for in this act. For the aforesaid purposes, the said fire department, or the superintendent of buildings, as the case may be, shall employ laborers and materials as may be necessary to perform said work as speedily as possible, and the city treasurer is authorized and directed to provide the funds to prosecute said work until completed. For the purpose of providing the money for said work and materials, or either of them, the city is hereby authorized to transfer to the order of the city treasurer such sums as may be necessary, from any unexpended or excessive appropriation of the then current or of any previous year, or to issue revenue bonds payable out of the taxes of the next ensuing year.

§ 62. This act is hereby declared to be a remedial statute, and is to be construed liberally to secure the beneficial interests and purposes thereof, Nothing herein contained shall be construed to affect any suit or proceeding now pending in any court, or any rights acquired, or liability incurred, nor any cause or causes of action accrued or existing, under any act repealed hereby; nor to repeal, limit or modify the powers and duties of any local or state board of health.

§ 63.   This act shall take effect ninety days after its passage.

www.ingramcontent.com/pod-product-compliance
Lightning Source LLC
Chambersburg PA
CBHW031247260626
47169CB00007B/2481